True North:
Tice's Story

Endorsements of Mark Alan Leslie's
Midnight Rider for the Morning Star:
From the Life and Times of Francis Asbury

"In a world of namby-pamby Christianity, along comes a story of a man who played no games with God. The life and exploits of Francis Asbury read like the biblical Book of Acts. Mark Alan Leslie did not write 'just another book.' I couldn't put *Midnight Rider for the Morning Star* down. Neither will you. This one is a 'must read.'"
— *Frank Eiklor, president,*
Shalom International

"…engaging, entertaining, informative and *convicting*. We spend so little time in God's Word, and have so little passion for souls! I am inspired by Asbury's life and example. Although I am one of our congregation's main evangelists, Bishop Asbury puts me to shame and challenges me to be more passionate, saltier, wiser, more effective at redeeming the time, and certainly more willing to suffer for the sake of the gospel."
— *Jamie Lash, Jewish Jewels,*
Fort Lauderdale, Fla.

"*Midnight Rider* is an exciting, exhilarating story that challenges the reader in an intense way."
— *Dr. Dennis E. Kinlaw, founder Francis Asbury Society and past president Asbury College*

"Again and again it spoke to my heart."
— *Merlin R. Carothers, founder
Foundation of Praise
and author of* From Prison to Praise

[It] is a stimulating and imagination-provoking book."
— *Patch Blakey, executive director,
Association of Classical and Christian Schools*

"An exhilarating historical novel, helping readers experience the heart and mind of this 'saint.'"
— *Chris Bounds, assistant professor
Indiana Wesleyan University*

"This is a fast-paced ride and read through the new Republic with America's most influential religious leader."
— *Darius Salter, church historian and pastor
Richardson (Texas) Church of the Nazarene*

"If the life of Francis Asbury ever inspires a movie, the script may resemble Mark Alan Leslie's historical novel, *Midnight Rider for the Morning Star*.
— *Bill Fentum, United Methodist Reporter*

"A delightful, enriching and inspiring read. The Church needs to read this and regain Asbury's passion and zeal. As a Christian and pastor, I've used this book for a witness several times."
— Pastor Randy Brown, Christian Revolution

True North: Tice's Story

A Novel
By Mark Alan Leslie

Gripfast Publishers

Copyright 2014 by Mark Alan Leslie
All rights reserved.

Cover by Loy Brackett Leslie, Monmouth, Maine
Photography by Mark Alan Leslie

This is a work of fiction. Though several names are historical characters, the specific actions in this book are products of the author's imagination.

Library of Congress Cataloging-in-Publication Data

Leslie, Mark Alan 1948-
True North: Tice's Story

ISBN: 9781628906028

All rights reserved. No part of this publication may be reproduced, stored in a retrieval system, or transmitted in any form or by any means—electronic, mechanical, digital, photocopy, recording, or any other—except for brief quotations in printed reviews, without the prior permission of the author.

In memory of the slaves who escaped their plantations, or died trying, and the thousands of people involved in the Underground Railroad who helped them along their way — oftentimes with significant threat to their own lives and fortunes.

Dedicated to Loy, my wife and partner in research about the heroes and heroines of a tumultuous time in our nation's history—one largely shaped for the good by the Christians of that day: the 1850s and 1860s.

Chapter One
The Year of Our Lord 1860

Tice stood at the banks of the swiftly flowing Ohio River, contemplating his future, or the end of it—the man with the gun chasing him close behind. Try to swim the river, he'd drown. Stay here, he'd get whipped half to death, or maybe all the way to death. That's what happened to runaway slaves.

Struggling to catch his breath, he thought, *Lord, how'd Your boy get here? What on earth I done?*

Like flipping the pages through a fast-moving picture book, the last hour or so of his life spun before his eyes. The day had begun so quietly, so drearily, like always.

There he was, maybe nineteen, twenty years old, standing with hoe in hand in his Massah's field, reflecting on his short life. This day like all the others. Still hackin' away in the dirt, still pickin' cotton, still sleepin' on a board.

He swung the hoe and joined in singing with the other slaves:

"Swing low, sweet chariot—"

Tice stood working in the cotton field, hoe in hand, singing with his fellow slaves, the words of the spiritual distracting him from the monotony of the chore that would consume his day. Singing helped. Sometimes the less you had on your mind, the better. Sometimes when you're not thinking of your Momma—God bless her soul—or your Pappy—*I hope you're still alive!*—the quicker the day goes. But today was different.

"Comin' for to carry me home—"

Tice's arms were swinging the hoe, his mouth was forming the words. But lately, his mind was on his Pappy and the freedom his father had whispered about to him a few summers ago, before being sold by Massah. Pappy had remembered that freedom with happiness.

"I looked o'er Jordan 'n what did I see—"

Tice continued working and singing, making his way across the field with the others under Massah's watchful eye. He had to keep up, do his share, or Massah would whip him, sure.

Just then, Massah gave a random crack of his whip, a frightening reminder of what he did to those who displeased him.

Tice struggled not to look toward the edge of the field, to the road where he'd met a stranger not two weeks prior.

The man had seemed to appear from nowhere, leaned down from his horse toward Tice and said quietly, "Young man, if you can ever escape, do so by crossing the Ohio River just south of the ferry and ask for the Randolph house. That's my place. Do that and we'll get you free. Remember that? Randolph?"

"A band o' angels comin' after me—"

Tice had nodded. *Randoaf.* He thought of another slave, a skinny old man the women called a "randy oaf."

He didn't know what that meant, but, as the man hurried off, Tice repeated, "Randoaf."

Since then, Tice had worked as usual. But the thought of escape stayed in the forefront of his mind, the taste of Pappy's freedom inhabiting his dreams at night.

"*Comin' for to carry me home.*"

Tice blinked hard twice, shook his head and nearly lost his grip on the hoe as he scolded himself. *Freedom 'n such is fool thinkin'.*

Suddenly, the whip smacked the ground by his feet and an icy hand laid firmly on Tice's bare shoulder. It sent a chill down his spine and cut the hymn short in his throat. His friends all around him in the cotton field took notice and stopped singing as well.

Clutching the neck of the hoe in his hands, as if to drain the life out of the wood, Tice turned an eye toward the firm grip and knew from the white, square-fingered hand whose it was.

"Yes-sir, Boss," Tice said, turning toward the man who owned him and another hundred slaves who toiled the fields as well as the plantation that spread for a mile in any direction. Tice dare not look his boss in the eye, so he focused on the man's chin.

"You're one of my strongest workers, Tice," Julius Lykins said, "so I need you to go down to the village, to the railroad station."

"Yes-sir, Massah Lykins."

"A shipment's arriving on the train. Morgan'll be down there, along with Gilly, waiting with a wagon. You get down there and help them unload."

Tice nodded.

"The shipment should arrive about the time you get there if you head out now. If you don't get there in time, you'll get the sting of this whip, boy." Lykins pushed his horse whip in front of Tice's eyes.

Tice cringed. He'd felt that sting before and had the welts across his back to prove it.

"Well, get on down there, boy. I expect you, Morgan and Gilly back here in an hour or so."

Tice handed his hoe to Elijah, his friend standing nearby, and started to quick-step out of the field toward the road to town.

"Clock's ticking, boy," his master said.

Tice started jogging.

"Tick tock!"

Tice set out in a full run, his hardened bare feet unaffected by the hard-packed dirt as he reached the road to the quiet Kentucky town of Maysville.

"Gotta get there or feel the whip. Gotta get there or feel the whip," Tice repeated to himself. As he ran, his brief life flashed across his mind. He was born on this plantation and knew nothing else. His Momma died of fever when he was a boy. A few years later his Pappy was sold to another plantation who knows where. He had no brothers or sisters, except brothers and sisters in the Lord.

An' here I is, still livin' for nothin'—'cept my relationship with my Lord. Here I is, runnin' into town for my Massah, goin' to load my Massah's stuff for my Massah's plantation, for my Massah's farm animals maybe, or my Misses's parlah.

The hymn lingered in his mind.

"If you get there before I do—"

Someday he'd have a manshun, he thought, a big old house in the sky. But until then, he was hoein' 'n pickin' 'n runnin' 'n loadin' here on earth for a man who beat him 'n his friends for fool reasons, or no fool reason t'all.

Tice was a speedy runner when need be and soon he looked up to see the rail station ahead. Sure enough, he could see the steam from the engine floating skyward, drifting side to side—same as he'd like to do. He began to sprint, not wanting Morgan, his Massah's foreman, to get upset with him. Morgan packed a more powerful whip than his Massah when his Massah wasn't watching.

"Comin' for to carry me home—"

Shortly Tice reached the train and saw Morgan talking to a man wearing a funny-looking hat. Gilly, another slave, stood behind Morgan. The man motioned to another fellow, who reached up and tugged at a rope on a door on the train, then slid the door open. Tice ran to Morgan's side and lowered his eyes to Morgan's chin.

"Let's get to it, boy," Morgan said. A burly man, Morgan twisted his handlebar mustache with a forefinger and thumb. "Hop up there and hand down the boxes to Gilly. He'll pass 'em to me and I'll load 'em up on the wagon."

"Yes-sir."

Tice sprang onto the train. Box upon box filled the rail car. What was in the boxes, he didn't know at first. Soon he discovered, though, from the sheer weight of them, that the cargo was dishes, plates, pots and pans and such items for the mansion. *This'll mean the manshun's* old *pots and pans for us-uns, maybe.*

In short order, Tice passed the last box to Gilly, a big fellow slave Tice hardly knew—indeed, nobody hardly knew 'cause he hardly spoke. A grunt here and a grunt there defined Gilly.

Loading the boxes onto the wagon and then strapping them down with rope, Morgan turned to Tice. "Gilly'll ride with me. No room for three. You'll hafta walk, boy. But don't ya' be dallyin'."

Tice liked that idea. He'd step along the side of the road where it was grassy and cooler under the shadow of the trees. He began the walk back and watched the wagon disappear ahead of him. As he stepped one foot in front of the other, a thought began to ferment in his mind. An exciting idea. An educated person who knew about epiphanies might call it one of those.

He looked up. Morgan and Gilly had disappeared over a rise in the road. Tice stopped in his tracks and repeated to himself, "Randoaf."

He glanced around him. Was anybody watching? Maybe the workers at the train station? No. Anyone ridin' or walkin' down the road? No.

"Tell all my friends I'm comin' too—"

Quickly, he set his feet to motion toward the plantation. Then, a hundred yards up the road, looking again to make sure no one was watching, Tice veered into the woods, eastward toward the Ohio River.

Pushing branches out of his face, Tice plowed through a woodland. "South of the ferry. Randoaf." His destination was etched in his mind. He knew the river. He knew where the ferry left Maysville and floated over to Ripley, Ohio, north of the Mason-Dixon Line, separating slave states from free states.

"Comin' for to carry me home."

As he hustled towards the land of freedom, doubts about that very liberty filled his mind. Sure, he'd be free. But where would he sleep? What would he eat? What work would he do—*could* he do? Who would be responsible for all this—all of him? First his Momma, then his Pappy and always—yes, always—Lykins saw to it that his hunger, thirst and shelter were taken care of. Now Momma was gone, Pappy was gone and he was leavin' Lykins.

Oh, Massah. Tice thought of more than one whipping at the hands of Lykins. At that memory, he hastened his steps, remembering Lykins saying he expected Tice back to the plantation soon. *When I doesn't arrive, Massah'll be furious 'n he'll come lookin' for me, and he'll have that whip in his hand. Oh, that whip!*

Several minutes later, he pushed another branch out of his face and came to a meadow. Nothing planted here. No cotton. No tobacco. Tice hesitated and looked around slowly, wanting to make sure no one would spot him if he made a mad dash across the field.

"South of the ferry. Randoaf," he muttered aloud as he sprang into the meadow at a speed that even surprised him. "South of the ferry. Randoaf."

Hay in the field tickled his ankles, but his focus remained on the river. Just then he heard a loud voice hollering, "Hey, you!"

It was a white man's voice. "You there!"

He pretended not to hear the man and continued to run.

"Stop your runnin', boy!"

Stop? Could he stop now? Doubts flooded in again.

He hesitated. Yes, he could stop. Maybe that would keep him out of trouble. Maybe the man wouldn't tell his Massah. Then he wouldn't have to worry about food on the table, a roof over his head, chores to do. No. No worries. He slowed down but didn't look in the direction of the voice.

What should he do? What would Pappy do? he asked himself. Then again he remembered his Pappy talking to him about being free until neighboring tribesmen raided his village, tied them up, then sold the whole village to a white man on a boat. Tice remembered the smile on his Pappy's face when he talked about being a free man, and he speeded up his pace again.

"Comin' for to carry me—"

"Stop or I'll shoot!"

Chills went down Tice's back. His knees almost buckled. Shoot? The man had a rifle? *Well, maybe dyin' wouldn't be bad, neither, Lord—compared to hoein' someone else's fields for the rest of my life.* He hurried on as fast as he could and finally reached the end of the pasture. No lead bullet was fired, only a missile of fear.

Tice dove into the forest, landing on the ground and rolling into a bramble bush. "Ouch!" he screamed, looking down in pain as blood began to leak out of his right arm. He gingerly pulled his arm away from the bush and touched his forearm. "Ow!"

He heard the man call to someone else, "Hurry up and tell Mister Lykins that I think one of his slaves is runnin' away toward the river! I'm chasin' after him!"

"Chasin' after him," Tice repeated. Oh, no. Hurry, he told himself. South of the ferry. Randoaf.

He pushed himself off the ground to his feet, got his bearings and ran off. How long could he go? How long had it been? Was Lykins missing him already? If not, that man was going to tell him. Fear rippled through him like tendrils of ice as Tice thought of the consequences of being caught.

"Dear Momma," he called out. "Dear Pappy. Save me."

"Dear Lord!" he said louder as he came to a hillock, "Where's my band o' angels?" He looked up and the top of the hillock appeared a mile away even though it was only probably fifty yards. "Oh, Lord, help me!"

Tice clambered up the mound. Was this the Blue Ridge Mountains? he wondered. He'd heard stories and thought they were far beyond the river. Was his mind workin' okay?

Just when his legs gave out, he reached the top of the hill. Falling to the ground, he looked up and saw the river in the distance. He took a few seconds to rest and draw his breath, knowing he couldn't wait long; the man was chasing after him. The man! Tice turned to look behind him. The man was nearing the base of the hillock!

"Stop right there!" The man scowled and pointed a

finger at Tice. "Stop there and it may spare you a beatin'!"

Tice shook his head. He knew that weren't true. *Not true t'all. I's long past bein' spared no beatin'. A beatin's a comin'. A bad beatin'—if'n I gets caught. If'n.*

The thought of the whip spurred him on, giving him a second wind, and he hustled down the hill, ducking away from alder branches along the way. He reached the bottom and skirted around another bramble bush. *Gotta get distance. Gotta get distance 'tween me 'n him. A long way.* He didn't see that the man had a rifle, but maybe he did.

Suddenly he splashed through a brook, his toes hit a rock and he fell to the bank of the brook, screaming in pain. He grabbed for his big toe. Had he broken it? He sat up and held his foot. Blood seeped out of his big and second toes. He put his foot back in the water, hoping the coolness would help numb it.

But he couldn't wait, couldn't linger a second longer. The man must be nearing the top of the hill by now and might spot him. His Pappy's face flashed before him. *"Git ov'r it, son. Buck up! Git up and run!"*

"Yes, Pappy," Tice said aloud. He lifted himself out of the water, stepped up to dry ground and set out running again as fast as he could while trying not to touch ground with those two injured toes.

And here he was, several minutes later, wheezing for breath, a sharp pain in his ribs, standing at the riverbank, fixated on the spring runoff streaking past in a maniacal race downstream. Yep. The choice: certain death or certain torture. Here was his future, or the end of it

Struggling to catch his breath, Tice said aloud, "Dear Pappy, save me!"

Chapter Two
At the River

Finally, drawing a deep breath, Tice slid down the riverbank and put his feet in the water, which almost swept him off his feet it was moving so fast. Grabbing a branch of a tree, he steadied himself and felt the water's coolness. *Oh, blessed coolness.* It helped numb his aching toes. Tice lay back on the bank, his chest heaving, and tried to calm his heavy breathing.

He closed his eyes for a few seconds, thinking, "South of the ferry. Randoaf. South of the ferry. Randoaf."

Tice turned his head and looked north up the river, where he spotted the ferry. It was coming over from the other side. That's when he saw, at the ferry landing, the white hat of his Massah. Or was it? The ferry was probably a hundred yards away over rough terrain.

Tice squinted to see if it was indeed Lykins. The man was the right size. The man wore a white hat. And the man carried a whip—a whip *and* a gun!

At that very moment, as if drawn by Tice's concentration, the man looked toward him. Tice ducked behind a bush on the riverbank, praying he wasn't spotted. Was he? Tice couldn't contain his curiosity and looked up slowly, peering around the shrub. The man had straightened his shoulders, turned fully downriver and was looking intently in Tice's direction—directly at him! Pointing his whip, the man hollered. He was far enough away that Tice didn't understand the words, but he could guess close enough.

A whippin', sure 'nough. A whippin'—or a hangin', or a shootin'!

Tice stood to swim into the river and then the thought struck him again, this time like a stone. He couldn't swim. Couldn't swim a lick! Couldn't swim across that brook he'd just run through. He looked across the river and guessed it was fifty yards or so to the other side. He wasn't sure, but it was forever away. Forever!

Tendrils of fear rattled up his spine, taking hold of his shoulders.

"Oh, my God, my God, my God," Tice prayed and dove into the river. He felt like a very big, very strong hand had pushed him forward. He came to the surface gasping for breath. Instead, water filled his mouth and he coughed it out, turning away from the flow of the river, gagging and flailing his arms.

I'm gonna die. Die right here in this here river and float right along, meat for some big fish—like Jonah's big fish. Suddenly that thought wasn't so bad as he compared it to facing Lykins' whip, and he calmed. Calmed down enough that he stopped flailing and found himself carried along, and atop, the river.

Engulfed in an odd startled tranquility, Tice looked over his shoulder toward the ferry. He could barely see a white hat, that was all. Apparently Lykins had decided to take the ferry to the other side of the river rather than run down the riverbank to shoot him.

The ferry! He strained to see where the ferry was and guessed it was approaching the landing where

Master stood, perhaps five or ten feet away. At that point, he remembered seeing one of his friends swim in a creek one day. He recalled the stroke of the arm, the kick of the feet. And he started to replicate them. Immediately he noticed he was advancing toward the other side of the river and he began a steady progress.

Closer and closer he came to the riverbank. Less and less he could feel his limbs. His arms felt like lumps, his legs like dead limbs of a tree. *Dear Lord. Dear Lord!* he pleaded. *Help yo' chil'. Help this son o' your'n.*

Just as Tice thought he could not swim another stroke, he reached the riverbank. Fighting the pull of the water, he grabbed hold of a branch of a small bush and tugged as hard as he could until his feet reached ground.

He looked intently upstream and saw the ferry halfway toward his side of the river. That sent an adrenaline rush that propelled him five feet almost straight up, to the top of the riverbank. The village of Ripley was nearby and he ran as fast as his wobbly legs could carry him. Weaving between trees, Tice repeated his would-be rescuer's name to himself. "Ran—Ron—Run?"

Tice stopped at a large oak tree and leaned against it. "Rin—Run—what was it?" Lacking oxygen, his brain couldn't recall the man's name. *It had somethin' to do with an old slave at the plantashun. Somethin', but what? Somethin' the women said about him. An old poop? Ranpoop? Was that it? No. No.*

Anxiously, he looked upriver through a grove of trees and could see the ferry was within a few feet of the landing. And, sure enough, Master was on board and getting ready to leap onto the landing as soon as it was within reach. Master with a whip in one hand, a rifle in the other and with Morgan at his side. Morgan, too! *Oh, Lord, help this chil'!*

Suddenly a cool breeze swept over Tice's body and with it came what he sought: Randoaf.

"That's it!" Tice said, looking heavenward. "Thank you, Lord!"

He turned and ran toward the nearest house, a blue two-story home encircled by a white picket fence. He surprised himself by leaping over the three-foot-high fence, then reached the rear door. Knocking on it, he thought to himself, What do I ask? What can I say? "I'm a law-breakin' slave; hide me"?

A moment later, an older white woman opened the door. To Tice, it appeared that the woman's wrinkly face nearly exploded with fear and agitation. Then he thought what she was looking at: a ragged, wet, bleeding—and petrified—young black man.

The only thing he could think to say blurted out of his mouth. "Randoaf?"

"Do you mean 'Randolph'?" the woman asked.

Tice hesitated. Master and Morgan must be walkin' down this road right now! He shrugged his shoulders. He didn't have time for this. The Lord had surely reminded him. Yes-sir, he remembered the randy oaf. "Randoaf," he repeated. "My Massah's comin' down the street. I gotta hide!"

"Come in here, young man. You're dripping wet." The woman took his hand and pulled him inside the house.

A white woman dared to touch me! Cared to touch me!

"Quickly!" she almost whispered and hurried down a hall and then up a staircase. Tice didn't have time to take measure of the home, even to gauge the wealth, or lack thereof, of its owner. But, looking out a window as he reached a landing halfway up the staircase, he did notice Massah knocking on the front door of the neighboring house. He stopped long enough to see Morgan on the other side of the street, with the familiar twisting of the handlebar mustache. The image of his Pappy suffering an awful whipping came to mind. "Oh, my, Lord," escaped Tice's lips.

Reaching the top of the staircase, the woman motioned to him. "In here," she said, pointing toward a door. "Quickly. It's a closet, but just stay quiet in there until I come to get you."

Tice hurried to her and stepped inside.

"Don't move!" she said, her eyes flashing. Then she shut the door and all went black on Tice.

Total darkness surrounded him. And utter quiet. He moaned softly and sank to the floor, sitting on his buttocks.

Coattails, apparently, rubbed on his head and, suddenly cold, he shivered. His arm ached where the brambles cut into the skin. His toes throbbed from being stubbed on the rocks. How he would like to wrap himself in a warm coat or dry himself off, but he didn't dare move for fear he would make a noise. He figured this closet was exactly above the front door, and if Massah came to this door and heard Tice muckin' about in this closet, he'd figure out it was him, for sure. Massah was a smart man. Tice didn't know about this old white woman, whether she was smart enough to outsmart Massah.

Lord, give her smarts, Tice thought. Make her smarter'n Massah.

•••••

Downstairs, plantation owner Julius Lykins knocked on the door of widow Jayne Weiss, who opened it, greeting him with a wide smile that momentarily disarmed him.

"Ma'am," he said, tipping his hat.

"Good morning," she said. "May I help you, sir?"

"I hope so, ma'am. My name's Julius Lykins. I own a plantation in Maysville and I'm after one of my slaves who's run away."

A very polite man, Jayne thought, but carrying a whip and a rifle.

"I've heard of you, Mister Lykins," she said. "You do realize you've crossed the Mason-Dixon Line."

"That I do, ma'am," Lykins said. "And you realize Congress has passed the second Fugitive Slave Law declaring that runaway slaves must, by decree, be returned to their masters and that citizens here shall not harbor and abet fugitives. My slave is a fugitive. He has run away. He is mine."

"Oh, dear sir, I *am* aware of the Fugitive Slave Law." Again Jayne smiled broadly at Lykins.

"And are you aware that under that law, anyone hiding a slave or helping him escape may be fined one thousand dollars or imprisoned for six months?"

"Yes, I am, and I'm afraid I can't help you, Mister Lykins."

"Are you aware that a man in Baltimore has been sentenced to forty-five years in jail for helping a family of nine slaves escape?"

"I have indeed read about that and, yet, I still cannot help you, sir."

Lykins frowned down at her and tightened his jaw. Following his eyes, Jayne noticed splotches of water along the hallway and leading up the steps of the staircase. Suddenly Lykins leveled a hard look at her.

"Spring a leak in a bucket, did ya'?"

Jayne's brow tightened.

"I—I'm sure it's nothing," she stammered.

Suddenly a drop of water, having dripped from Tice and worked through the second-story floorboards, fell straight down between her and Lykins. Both watched it as if it were falling in slow motion. Two seconds later, another drop fell.

Jayne said nothing, but prayed silently.

"I think you've sprung a leak by God and it's not from a bucket," Lykins said. He put a hand to her shoulder to push her aside. "I'd better go upstairs and help you with that."

Jayne mustered her courage, planted her feet and resisted. "Sir," she said, "you will do nothing of the sort, and especially 'by God,' for He is my God."

"Oh, I think I shall." Lykins stepped past her toward the staircase. As he did, he lifted the rifle to his shoulder.

"One step further and I'll call my son." For a little woman the words carried an especially menacing tone.

Lykins smiled devilishly at her. "You do that, ma'am."

"My son, Constable Jacob Weiss," she said, "who would arrest you for trespassing and aggravated assault on an old woman!"

Lykins stopped in his tracks. Her son the constable. And a Jew to boot. He'd heard of this trouble-making Weiss. He swore.

"And I'll be obliged if you didn't take the Lord's name in vain in my house." Jayne crossed her arms and looked at him like a school teacher at an unruly student.

Lykins eyed her keenly, then turned and walked slowly back to the doorway. Locking his eyes on hers, he pointed a finger at her from the hand that held the whip. "I'm going to find that slave, and you'd better pray I don't prove you're hiding him in your house, or *I'll* be the one calling your son the constable."

"I'd be obliged if you'd take your whip, your rifle and your bony finger and leave these premises," Jayne said.

Lykins gave her a peevish look and turned on his heels. Once outside the door, he gazed over his shoulder at her, spit on the ground and stalked off.

Disgusted, Jayne closed the door. A small table at the foot of the staircase drew her attention. Placing her hand on the worn leather cover of the Tanach, which lay on it, she said, "My law is a higher law than the Compromise Bill, mister plantation owner. A much higher law."

Above her, Tice sat with his arms wrapped about him, shivering. Shivering both from the cold and the fright he was just now calming down. He had heard the entire conversation, felt every nuance and, familiar with the menace of his Massah, now knew something of the character of this little old white woman.

Chapter Three
1860 in Ripley, Ohio

Tice shivered in the closet. It was dark. He was cold. His arm and toes hurt like the dickens. And it was cramped space for his six-foot-tall body, no matter how lean he was.

Lord, he prayed, I'm none of a person for you to care for, I knows that. But I knows You care for the little sparrows, so I knows you care for me, 'gardless.

He heard footsteps ascending the staircase and pulled his legs tight against his bottom, thinking if Lykins opened the closet door perhaps he could become invisible to him.

Lord, make me so Massah can't see me. Please!

Tice pulled his head down between his shoulders and closed his eyes. The closet door squeaked on its hinges as it opened, ever so slowly, too slowly for Tice.

"Young man?" The voice was like that of an angel to Tice's ears. He let out the breath he had been holding for some time. Not Massah! No, it was the old woman. The old, white woman.

Suddenly the question came to his mind. After all this runnin' an' chasin' an' hidin', Tice wondered, Why would a young white man and an old white woman care to rescue me?

"Come with me, young man." Jayne reached down with her hand. He hesitated, then took it and rose to his feet.

"Now, listen. You have to be quiet and you have to watch that no one sees you. Eyes and ears are everywhere on the lookout for runaways."

Tice nodded.

"That man looking for you—" Jayne put her hand to Tice's chin and raised his head so he was looking at her. Startled again that she would want him to look directly at her, Tice did and that's when he noticed the sincerity, the concern, the love in her face. "That man is not going to go away. He, or one of his foremen, will be keeping an eye on this house and so we have to move you on."

He nodded again.

"But first we have to get you dried and warm and see if we can get some other clothes for you to wear."

Tice shivered again and looked down at what he was wearing. These were new pants for him, only a couple years old. He had kept growing and growing and pants had kept getting' too short and short still. And finally, these fit pretty good, coming even with his ankles. No, this weren't no new shirt but it had all its buttons—well, 'cept the top two—and maybe there was a tear or two along the short sleeves, but it kept him pretty much covered.

Jayne was at the top of the staircase. She turned to him. "What's your name, young man?"

He stammered. "Tice, ma'am."

"Tice. A different name. I like it." She nodded firmly. "It's Tice, then. They call me Miss Jayne, though I'm a widow. Jayne Weiss."

Not call her just "misses" or "ma'am"?

"Follow me, Tice, and duck down low when you

come to the window at the landing. We don't want anyone to see you inside here."

Tice did as told, following Jayne down the stairs, along the hallway and into a bedroom. There she handed him a towel. "Take off your clothes, dry yourself off and I'll be back."

As Tice shook out the towel, he noticed Jayne assessing him before she left, mentally measuring his frame. She bowed her head and a sad smile wrinkled her face.

•••••

Soon afterwards, Jayne returned to the room, holding up clothes to him.

"My husband, Joseph, was a tall, slender man, too," she said. "He loved the story of the our people, the Hebrew slaves, and their exodus from Egypt. He would have been proud to let a young, runaway slave wear his clothes in which to escape to freedom."

Tice simply smiled and accepted the pants and shirt as well as socks and shoes.

Two hours later, his belly full of chicken, beans and potatoes, Tice listened to Jayne's instructions.

"There's a man standing across the street behind a tree, watching the house and thinking I don't know he's there. The good Lord showed him to me," she said.

Tice nodded, his eyes widening a bit. Morgan!

"We're going to fool him," Jayne went on. "I'm going to go out the front door, walk right up to him and engage him in a bit of talk about the ills of one person 'owning' another and such."

"Like Massah 'n me?"

"Yes, Tice. But may no man ever be your 'master' again." She raised a finger, but it was one of instruction not a bony finger of condemnation like his Massah's.

Tice smiled broadly.

"My people, the Jews, are familiar with being slaves. But we escaped Egypt with God's help, and Babylon, too. No, never again. And never again for you, either.

"Now," she continued, "when I get to that man, I'm going to stand at his side so he'll have to turn to face me. When he does, I want you to crawl out the side window in the parlor. Keep in mind, there may be someone out back in the woods watching, too; the Lord didn't tell me about him if there is. But keep close to the ground and run as fast as you can."

Jayne gave him directions to Alden Randolph's house, which was just a couple of hundred yards away.

"While you were eating, I had my grandnephew deliver a message to Alden Randolph, so he and his wife, Mindy, will be expecting you. Go to the rear door where the tall bucket full of cat-o-nine-tails stands. Knock twice, wait a second, then knock once."

Tice nodded. He liked the idea of escaping but already missed this lady, the tender touch of her hand on his, the love in her eyes. He didn't look forward to the fear he knew would grip at him when he climbed out the window, the panic like that which gnawed at his nerves all the while he ran from Maysville to the Ohio River just hours ago.

Jayne smiled, leaned down and kissed him on the forehead. "The Lord go with you, Tice."

"Thank you, ma'am. I sure hope He does!"

At that, Jayne left the kitchen and walked up the hall and out of the house. Tice stepped to the parlor, where he could see through a window in the living room at the front of the house. Sure enough, Miss Jayne walked right up to the man. And it was Morgan. And, sure enough, she addressed him from the north, so that Morgan, twisting his handlebar mustache with a forefinger and thumb, turned to face her.

Tice wondered what she was saying as he moved swiftly to the parlor window and opened it. *What's she sayin' that will keep his attenshun away from me?*

Tice slipped a leg out the window and then his second leg and dropped the few inches to the ground. *'Crawl like a snake on 'is belly, so's no one can see ya'.*

He dropped to the ground and moved like a short-legged spider through low grass—*anyone lookin' from the woods?*—to the back yard of the neighboring house. *Nope, no one or they'd be hollerin'.* When he felt safely behind the house, he raised himself to a crouch and took off running through another backyard, then another with just a sliver of a moon shining faint light upon the ground around him so that he had to dodge several trees. Then, suddenly, he noticed a gas light at the back of a big, big house. The light was at a door and below it stood a big pail full of cat-o'-nine-tails.

"Randoaf!" he said to himself.

He raced to the door and knocked twice, waited a couple seconds and rapped on it once more.

He looked himself over in the light. *I wonder if Misser Randoaf'll recognize me in these here clothes.* He hardly recognized himself, what with a nice clean shirt with all its buttons and pants that were pretty new and only a little too short for his long legs. The only thing Miss Jayne didn't have for him to wear was shoes. His big feet couldn't fit in her husband's shoes. Besides that, he didn't think they'd be comfortable anyway.

Suddenly the door opened and Alden Randolph stuck his head out. "Come in. Come in," he whispered hastily.

Tice stepped inside but couldn't see much. A lone candle lit the room in which they stood. It was the kitchen, obviously that of a rich man. Tice wondered if Randolph had slaves of his own. The thought leaped up at him: *Maybe he's jus' tryin' to steal away Massah's slaves! What if...*

"What's your name, son?"

Tice's thoughts were interrupted by the man. Randolph was extending his hand toward Tice's. "Mine's Alden."

Tice hesitated. Here was another white person willing to touch him. Someone else besides that sweet grandmother. His hand shaking, Tice reached forward and Randolph gripped it heartily. "Tice," he said. "They calls me Tice."

"We're thrilled you could make it, Tice. My wife, Mindy, is upstairs making up a bed for you to sleep in. We've kept the lights off because Miss Jayne informed us a man is looking for you here and we don't want him to see you through the windows."

Tice nodded.

"It's against the law for us to harbor you, Tice, so we have to be very, very careful."

"Harbor?" The word was foreign to Tice.

"Hide. Conceal. Help you get away."

"'scape," Tice said.

"Exactly. But we're going to do just that, my friend."

Tice smiled broadly. The girls at the plantation told him he had a wonderful smile, and when it was dark they couldn't see him but always could see his smile, which made them smile, too. So he decided to flash it to this man.

"Follow me, Tice. I'll take you up to your room. Try to keep in the shadows."

They went through a couple of rooms and then up a flight of stairs, then up another flight of narrower stairs. At the top was a little door that Tice had to duck to get through.

Inside, two candles shined brightly and the prettiest white woman Tice had ever laid eyes on stood before them.

She smiled at him.

"Mindy, this is Tice," Alden said.

Mindy nodded. "We're so glad you're here, Tice. Here's your bed for the night." She swept an arm toward a single-size bed with a mattress, covered with sheets and a quilt.

Tice was taken aback. He'd never had a mattress before. He didn't even know what it was called. He looked around, wondering why they were unconcerned about the bright light. The only window was covered by a thick blanket.

"No one can see the light up here," Alden said. "They'll be looking for you tomorrow, all around town. But they won't get any help. Not here. Not in Ripley."

"We're good Godly people here and slavery has no part in this place," Mindy Randolph joined in, adding firmly, "No man should own any other man."

"I sure wouldn't wanna own nobody," Tice said.

"Tice," Alden said, "we want you to get a good night's sleep. We want to get you on your way as soon as possible, but you may have to hide here for a few days. It all depends on how closely your master's having the town watched."

"Morgan's here!" The words escaped unrestrained out Tice's mouth.

"Is that the man across the street from Miss Jayne's?"

"Yes-sir, an' he's a dan'gous man. Dan'gous! When he's whippin', he's whippin angry. Angry!"

Alden and Mindy both winced at his words.

• • • • •

The next morning, Tice awoke in bed after a night's sleep bombarded by dreams. He was running and Morgan and Massah were chasing. Once he was way ahead of them, but then he got stuck in mud. Mud thicker than pudding and to his knees. And though the mud didn't cover a great area, his progress through it was tormenting, slow. Nearby trees grabbed at him, their branches like long arms, their twigs like bony fingers, reaching, reaching. Twice he woke up in a sweat, not sure if he had screamed in real life or in the dreams.

Finally, Tice prayed to the Lord for good dreams and he was able to get back to a calm sleep. His father appeared to him. "Ticey," he said softly, "come sit on your Pappy's lap." His father patted his thigh.

Pappy doesn't call me "Ticey" no more 'n I'm too big for this, Tice thought, but he did as Pappy said and noticed that he was a little boy. Pappy's lap was comfortable. He leaned into his Pappy's chest and his father wrapped his big arms around him. Bigger, stronger arms than anyone else—anyone. Tice felt secure, protected, so good he didn't want it to end. So good that he fell asleep—warm and comfortable, safe and secure, with no bad men chasing him. It was so good.

A knock at the bedroom door awoke him.

"Tice?" Words tripped out of Mindy Randolph like the sweet voice of Isabelle, his favorite "auntie" who sang hymns while she picked cotton. Tice could see Isabelle's face and he wondered if she was praying for him today, praying for his escape. "Tice, are you up?"

"Sittin' up in bed," he said, rubbing his eyes with his knuckles.

"I'll be back in a minute with your breakfast. Mister Randolph is out checking to see if your master's man is around the village before we can bring you downstairs."

"Thank you, ma'am." Tice swung his feet out of bed and dressed. A minute later, Mindy arrived with a tray filled with food. Scrambled eggs, fried bacon, toasted bread. *A feast for a massah!*

And so it was, for a week, with Tice living in the attic hideaway and coming downstairs only to sneak to the two-holer outhouse in the shed attached to the back of the house. Mindy delivered all the meals and visited with Tice during the day, learning about his life at the plantation, about his parents, his dreams, what work he knew how to do. And she even started to teach him how to read.

"You'll need to read in order to reach your dreams, Tice," she said, using a huge Bible to teach him the letters and how they sounded. In three short days he learned a lot. He knew because Mindy told him how intelligent he was. He remembered his Momma telling him how smart he was and so he smiled broadly at this nice white woman. By now, of course, he didn't consider Mindy Randolph white, black or yellow—just a very nice lady with a soft voice who laughed easily, encouraged mightily and felt like family.

One day she read to him from Psalm 59:

"Deliver me from my enemies, O God; protect me from those who rise up against me. Deliver me from evildoers and save me from bloodthirsty men.

See how they lie in wait for me! Fierce men conspire against me for no offense or sin of mine, O Lord. I have done no wrong, yet they are ready to attack me. Arise to help me; look on my plight!"

Mindy, who was sitting in a chair in the attic room, looked at Tice, who sprawled on his bed. "David wrote this psalm when Saul, the king, had sent men to watch David's house in order to kill him," she said.

The reason Mindy read the psalm suddenly dawned on Tice. "Like Morgan watchin' for me."

"Exactly," Mindy said. "But do you know how David ends the psalm?"

Tice shook his head.

Mindy read on:

"But I will sing of your strength, in the morning. I will sing of your love; for you are my fortress, my refuge in times of trouble.

O my Strength, I sing praise to you; you, O God, are my fortress, my loving God."

"Tice, let's pray together, that the Lord will deliver you to safety from these evil men and from this menace of slavery."

"Yeah!" he said eagerly.

Mindy reached out to take his hands in hers and bowed her head.

•••••

Meanwhile, Alden Randolph was gone most of the day every day. He owned a lumber mill and couldn't stay at home much.

Being out about town, he learned about Morgan's search for the missing slave.

"Boy's treacherous!" Morgan was telling everyone who would listen. "You see or hear anything 'bout him, you let me know, ya' hear?"

Alden recalled Tice calling Morgan 'dangous' and decided he believed Tice more than this angry-looking man who carried a whip wherever he went.

He wasn't the only one siding with the runaway. These villagers had helped a dozen or more slaves escape. Not one of them was pro-slavery as far as Alden knew, and he knew them all well since he was born in and grew up in Ripley.

Nevertheless, Morgan was persistent, slithering around town from morning to night, keeping a sharp eye on the houses. Alden was informed that a couple of times Morgan traveled north and northeast, trying to catch Tice's trail in those directions. But of course there was no trail to discover.

•••••

On the eighth morning Alden knocked at the third-story door.
Tice invited him in.
"Tice, tonight's the night," Alden said.
Tice looked questioningly at him.
"The night we get you out of here to your next safe house."
"Safe house?"
"The next home, north and east of here, where people will feed and protect you until they, too, can get you further on your way."
Tice thought of that 'way,' a journey Alden and Mindy had both spoken of to him. It sounded like Canaan-land, he thought, a place of milk 'n honey like Moses led the chillun of God to when they 'scaped from the Gyptchuns.
No one in this Canaan-land cared a brick 'bout your skin color. They all treated you the same. You could work 'n earn money for food 'n a place to live. Freedom. That's it. They should call it Freedom-land, though Misser Alden told him it was called "New Brunswick" and "Can'da."
Well, to Tice it would be "Freedom-land," and to Tice that would be the end of the rainbow. The way Alden described Can'da, it didn't sound much like how Tice's father described 'frica, but at least it didn't include Massah or Morgan or anyone else with a whip.

"I'm gonna miss you 'n Misses," Tice said solemnly.

Alden smiled. "We'll miss you, too, Tice. Actually, I wish you could stay here with us, work at my mill. But they'd catch you for sure and haul you back to the plantation, or perhaps just hang you."

Tice cringed at the thought. "I seen that done," he said, "the hanging man a-kickin' 'n a-squirmin'. That weren't no way to die."

"Tice, come with me," Alden said. "I want to show you a lesson God showed me about the black man and the white man. Okay?"

Tice dressed himself and followed Alden downstairs to the parlor, keeping clear of the windows on the way. Alden led him to a grand piano. Tice had heard Mindy play the instrument in the evenings. It sounded beautiful, prettier than anything he'd ever heard before. At least he had thought it was Mindy playing. Maybe it was Alden, or perhaps both of them.

As Mindy walked into the room to join them, Alden sat on the bench at the piano and patted the seat beside him. "Sit here, Tice."

When Tice had sat down, Alden said, "See the black and white keys?"

Tice nodded.

"Guess what, Tice. Your Negro spirituals—those beautiful songs you sing in the fields, the songs you sing to God, they're all played entirely on the black keys, these ones that stick up higher than the white ones.

With that, Alden played the first few bars of the spiritual *Swing Low, Sweet Chariot.*

"That's my favorite!" Tice yelped with joy.

"Really? Well, that song was written about this town where we live." Alden looked at Tice. "I understand you swam here."

Tice nodded agreement.

"Well, most of the escaping slaves get help from the townspeople who row boats to the other side of the river. That's why the spiritual says: 'I looked over Jordan and what did I see—coming for to carry me home. A band of angels coming after me.'"

"So's you's my angels," Tice said, showing his full set of teeth.

Mindy walked to him and gently squeezed his shoulder. "There's lots of them here, and lots more you'll meet once you leave."

Tice nodded again.

"Here's another of your spirituals," Alden said, and he began playing *The Gospel Train*.

Mindy began singing the words: "She is coming. Get on board. There's room for many more."

Tice thought her voice was just as melodious as Isabelle's. It must reach to the Lord's heaven.

"I love that one, too!" he said.

"Did you notice that I only touched the black keys?" Alden asked.

"Yes-sir."

"Do you know what that song, *The Gospel Train*, is about, Tice?" Mindy asked.

"No, ma'am."

"It's about the road you yourself, right now, are taking to freedom."

"Yeah?"

"Listen," Mindy said, "it says, 'She is coming. Get on board. There's room for many more.' That, Tice, is a direct call for your people to ride on out of the South."

Tice's eyes widened.

"Now listen," Alden cut in, "because I want to show you what can happen when black people and white work together. With that, his fingers took off playing the first stanza of *Glory Hallelujah* and using the full

31

range of black and white keys over three octaves.

Tice was stunned by the sound, its richness, how Alden's fingers flew over the keys using both hands at the same time and black and white keys together.

Alden stopped, letting the last sounds echo in the room.

"See what happens when you combine the black and white keys?" he asked.

"It's bu'ful," Tice said. "Fab'lis. I love it!"

"Well, that's God's plan for all of us, Tice. That's what He wants for His people, black and white. He wants us all worshipping Him together with no thought whatsoever of what is the color of our skin. It's a wonderful thing, just like the fullness of the sound of this piano is a marvelous result."

Tice now knew why these white people were helping him. They knew the same Lord he did, the God who said to love your neighbor as you love yourself, and so they loved him and knew the Lord wanted him to live in Freedom-land.

•••••

As night fell, Mindy Randolph set to putting together a daypack that included an extra shirt and trousers, along with a loaf of fresh bread, some smoked beef and the biggest slice of cheese Tice had ever seen. As Tice stood in the kitchen watching her, Alden stepped inside from the back door.

"Ready?" he asked.

Mindy tied a knot in the cloth that held all the provisions together. Sighing deeply, she said, "Ready."

With a happy smile that seemed slightly twisted by an odd sadness, she set down the daypack, which was tied to a thick pole, and stepped toward Tice. She wrapped her arms around him.

"You'll be in our prayers, daily and forever, Tice."

He hugged her back—hugged a white woman! "You, too, Misses—" he said, then read the turn of her head and corrected himself, "Mindy."

She stepped back and handed him his daypack. "God be with you."

Tice put the daypack over his shoulder, smiled one last time at her, then followed Alden out the door. Alden had snuffed out the outdoor lantern and there was only a half moon shining dimly on the earth, so Tice followed closely behind.

They walked quickly to a back door to the Randolphs' barn, where Alden had hitched up a horse and wagon.

"Hop in the back and pull some hay and the blanket over you," Alden instructed.

Tice followed directions and thoughts poured out. *Pappy, I did what you said. I ran, I swam and now I'm 'scapin'!*

The thrill of it sent chills down his spine.

A few minutes later, with Tice trying to get used to the jarring bumps lying in the wagon as it traveled over ruts in the dirt road, Alden spoke in a raised whisper. "Tice! There're two lights up ahead coming toward us. Stay still. Don't speak. Don't move!"

Oh, no! What's this? Tice pulled his knees up tight to his face and became as small as he could. And he prayed ever more vehemently. *O Lord, O Lord, 'tect Your chil, 'tect me! Make me invis'ble.*

Tice stopped breathing, or at least it seemed so, but listened intently.

Alden slowed his horse. Tice guessed they were outside the village by now, on the long road to Redoak, where Misser Alden had told him they were headin'. Tice listened intently. It sounded like two horses. He could see a dim light through the straw and blanket.

They's carryin' lanterns! 'N with light they can see me in this here buckboard!

Quiet as a church mouse, Tice thought to himself, then shivered as he thought he felt a little mouse run over his chest. *Oh Lord!* He almost jumped, then started praying even more fervently. *'Vis'ble to the world, Lord. Like a ghost.*

"Evenin', sir." The sound was muffled to Tice, but the voice was distinct. It was Morgan. Tice's hand began to shake.

The wagon stopped. Tice could hear the horses breathing and snorting. One whinnied, another nickered. Maybe they feel as antsy as me, Tice thought and for a moment he felt sorry for them. They didn't know what their massahs were up to, after all.

Then he heard Alden ask, "What are you men up to, stopping me here?" Tice remembered Alden placing a rifle on the bucket seat beside him and wondered if he was reached for it right now.

"No need for that there weapon." Yep, that there's Morgan, Tice confirmed. He could envision Morgan twisting that big ole mustache with a forefinger and thumb. Tice tried to move the blanket ever so slightly from his ear so he could hear better. "We're on the lookout for a runaway slave."

"Sorry. I can't help you there."

"What are you doing out in the middle of the night like this?"

"Not that it's any of your business, but I'm taking some medicine to a sick friend." Alden pulled a bottle out of Tice's daypack which was in the seat beside him. "Ayer's Sarsaparilla. For kidney problems."

"Well, it's certainly helped my appetite and digestion," Morgan chuckled. "Say, I wonder if we could take a look in the back of your buckwagon. You never know who can sneak into a man's wagon without his even knowin'."

"I think not." Tice couldn't tell for sure, but it sure sounded like Alden had cocked the rifle. Oh, no! Tice thought as he remembered one particular time when he saw a slave shot in the back while trying to run away when accused of speaking to Misses Lykins. The sound of that rifle cocking and bullet firing and the young slave falling dead haunted his dreams sometimes.

"It's not worth murder to you, is it?" That was Morgan's voice again.

Tice heard one of the horses slop up closer to the wagon, closer to Misser Alden. At the same time another horse rode to the other side. *Oh, Lord, help me ag'in.*

"Well, then," Alden said, with reluctance in his voice, "I've got nothing to hide."

•••••

While Morgan kept an eye on Alden, the second man, visible from the light from his lantern, converged on the wagon. He was a wiry-looking fellow with a long face and unkempt hair sticking out the brim of a wide hat. He hopped off his horse and, holding his lantern high in his left hand, moved the hay in the wagon with his right. Back and forth he moved it.

Finally, disgust in his voice, the little man said, "Nothin' here but hay and a blanket. What'cha got a blanket in there for, mister?"

Alden twisted to look behind himself, and a puzzled look came over his face. He wavered for a second. "Blanket?"

The little man swung the blanket out from under the hay. "Yes-sir, a blue blanket."

"Must've been one of my hired hands," Alden said. "I own Randolph's Lumberyard and my workers sometimes use my wagon."

"Maybe some fondlin' goin' on?" Morgan cut in.

Alden turned to look at him with aversion. "Not in my wagon. No."

The man chuckled scornfully. "Right-o, sir. Well, we'll be movin' on, then."

Alden set down his rifle, grabbed the reins in both hands and urged on his horse.

"Hope your friend's feelin' better," Morgan called after him.

Alden kept the wagon moving slowly.

•••••

Tice was glad for the slow speed. Right after his prayer to God, he had slithered out of the wagon like a squirmy little snake on his belly and slid out the back, then crawled under the buckboard, grabbed an axle and held on tight. From there he had listened as the fella searched for him.

Once he felt safely out of sight of Morgan, Tice dropped to the ground, let the wagon roll past, then jumped to his feet and rushed ahead. Grabbing hold of the wagon, he pulled himself up into the back.

"Tice!" Alden exclaimed.

Tice stepped forward into the seat beside Alden.

"I's vis'ble again," he whispered with a chuckle.

"What did you do?"

"I's layin' there prayin' and askin' the Lord to make me 'vis'ble 'n He says to me, 'Tice, you want to be 'vis'ble you slide on your tummy to the back of the wagon and then crawl under it and grab hold of the belly of this thing. Then pull yerself right tight up to it and hold on 'til I tell ya' t' let go.'"

Tice swiped sweat off his brow. "Wow! That was harder'n hoein' any field."

Alden smiled. "I think, for safety's sake, you should get back there under the hay and blanket again."

Tice obliged and hopped to the back.

"And Tice," Alden said, "when you thank the Lord, thank Him for me, too, will you?"

Tice nodded in agreement and when he got settled, Alden began to urge the horse on at a gallop. Good, Tice thought, the longer away from Morgan 'n that t'other man, the better. But maybe others are out on this road jus' like them 'tween me 'n Freedom-Land.

•••••

Tice lay in the back and fell fast asleep despite what had been the roughest ride of his young life.

It was four or five hours later that Alden pulled the horse up beside a house in the country and drove up to a large barn.

The horses stopping roused Tice from his slumber.

Alden turned and looked at him. "What a sleep you had despite the bumps. Now *that's* peace."

"Under His wing," Tice offered in explanation, then smiled the broadest smile he could muster.

"Come on up here with me," Alden said.

Tice hurriedly joined him. Before them, a barn door swung open and the silhouette of a man appeared in the moon-shadows of the structure.

"Pull it right in here," came Joseph Conrad's strong voice.

Shortly, with the wagon inside and the door closed, Alden introduced the men and Jonathan extended a hand to Tice. Getting used to the idea, Tice shook hands with him.

"I'm thankin' you, sir, for hidin' me out." He turned to Alden. "But I'm sure gonna miss you 'n Mindy."

"Well, Tice, when this whole slavery situation gets

taken care of, you have a job with me any time you want it."

Tice smiled.

"So, you'll be taking him north to the next stop?" Alden asked Jonathan.

His friend shook his head. "Got to change plans," he said. "There're a lot of slave hunters along the way north. I'll connect him to another route going east-northeast."

"Really?"

"Yep. Up through New York and Massachusetts to New Brunswick. We'll go that way until things calm down a bit on Africa Road."

Jonathan explained to Tice that Africa Road was the normal direct route to take north to Michigan and Canada. But slave hunters had discovered it. And, at the moment, the road through the crossroads of East Orange was too dangerous to travel.

"So your journey to freedom, Tice, will be a lot longer than I'd thought. I'm sorry."

Tice shrugged and smiled. "But I'm on my way—thanks to you."

Alden smiled and hugged him—hugged him tight.

Then Alden pulled the daypack down from the bucket seat and handed it to Tice along with an envelope. "There's some money in here to help you along the way, Tice. But be frugal."

"Frugal?"

"Careful with how you spend it."

"Yes-sir."

A minute later, Alden was on his way home and Jonathan was walking Tice into his farmhouse.

Chapter Four
Trekking Northeastward

Two months after Alden surreptitiously dropped Tice off at Jonathan Conrad's barn, Tice lived in a whirlwind. Never more than a few days in one place, he discovered that these white people actually liked him. It continued to be a revelation, though no longer as startling as when he had stepped into the widow Weiss's house after his dangerous swim across the Ohio River.

Tice learned to smile and simply be himself. He lost count of the families who had taken him in, sheltered him, fed him, then moved him on. Northeastward, forever northeastward.

All along the way his hosts continued to teach him to read. At one home in New York, a nice elderly spinster—"Maisey, dear boy, just call me Maisey," she said—read a different book with him. It was called *The Pilgrim's Progress*. The words were more difficult for Tice to understand, but she helped him with that.

"The man, called Pilgrim, is a lot like you, dear child," she said. Tice smiled at the thought of this little lady, a foot shorter than him, calling him "child."

"He's on a journey to the Kingdom of Heaven," she said. "On the way he encounters many obstacles, many people who are similar to what you may meet on your own journey. So it's good you learn from his experience because you may very well face similar situations—and people."

Tice nodded, waiting for her to go on.

"Pilgrim meets Discouragement, Depression, Hypocrisy and Worldly Wisdom—"

Oh, Tice knew disco'gement and 'pression, all right, but ... "Hip—" he tried to repeat the word.

"Hypocrisy," Maisey said. "It means being two-faced, not doing what you say you believe in, not being the person you make yourself out to be."

Tice had seen plenty of that on the plantation. Women slaves talkin' about other women slaves behind their backs; household slaves pretendin' to be friends with the field slaves but not really being friends t'all.

"Worldly Wisdom," she said, "that's one to be particularly wary of. That's the person who thinks they know what's best—for everyone including you."

"Uh-huh."

"And there's the Man of Stout Countenance, who forces his way into the Palace of Eternal Glory."

"Stout count—?"

"Big and strong."

"'N he beats up people to get what he wants?"

"Yes."

"Oh, that's Morgan, Masser's foreman!"

"A-ha. Well, dear boy, there are also people who are trustworthy, full of good will, hopeful and faithful."

"Mindy and Misser Alden," Tice said.

"Mindy and Alden?"

"The Randoafs," Tice said. "My friends over the river. Mindy's the one who started teachin' me t' read."

"Yes, yes," Maisey said. "God bless them. Well, in this book we'll read about Pilgrim's journey from the City of Destruction—"

"Oh, that's the plantashun!" Tice said.

"Yes, and through Doubting Castle—"

"'N that's like when I was swimmin' 'cross the river 'n didn't know how to swim!" Tice said.

"Really?" Maisey lit up and appeared to think about that for a long moment, then continued, "and going on to Mount Zion, God's home which here on earth is Jerusalem, the home of the Jews, but in our spirit it's Heaven."

"For me, that's Can'da, right?" Tice asked.

"Yes, Canada." Maisey folded her hands and looked directly up into Tice's eyes. Tice had no doubt that hers were eyes of love, true and deep.

"In the end," she said, "Pilgrim loses his burden at the Cross."

"Oh, I've lost that, ma'am." Tice's words bubbled with enthusiasm.

"Really?"

"Yes, somethin' my Pappy taught me when's I's a li'l tyke sittin' on his knee. Taught me about Jee—sus. What He done for us on that cross so's I can go to God and ask for forgiveness of all I done wrong."

"I see," Maisey said in a hushed tone. She placed a tiny hand on his and squeezed. "Then this book ought to be yours to have. Just as you learn to read, let it teach you along the way."

With that, she handed Tice her leather-bound copy of *The Pilgrim's Progress*. He determined he would treasure it the rest of his life.

•••••

Then one night in Norwich, Connecticut, a man named Wakeman—tall and tough but with sparkling blue eyes—came to the door of the home where Tice was hiding out.

"Quickly, son. Quickly!" Wakeman said as the

young couple who hid Tice pushed him out the door with a basket full of bread and cheese, the woman standing on her toes to kiss him on the cheek.

"Go with God," she said.

"Godspeed," her husband added.

"Yes, ma'am, sir." Tice's smile was fleeting as Wakeman grabbed his elbow and tugged him along to a low-slung wagon.

"Get in, son, and keep low," Wakeman said in a husky whisper.

"Yes-sir." With the basket in one hand and a bundle containing his clothing and his copy of *The Pilgrim's Progress* in the other, Tice jumped aboard. Looking back at the house, he noticed the lady was standing with head bowed. She was praying.

Wakeman whipped at the horse in a mad dash to the rail station in Norwich. *Boy, this is a fast, bumbly-kajingity-bangity-bangity ride!* Tice thought as he jounced along. It was just a couple miles from the couple's house, but Tice felt every bump as he lay silent in the buckboard.

Suddenly Wakeman pulled the wagon to a stop. "Hurry, son!" he said. "You have to catch this train!"

Tice grabbed his food and belongings and leaped to the ground. Wakeman pulled the wagon into a pasture, then jumped from the buckboard. "Follow me," he said as he ran ahead. *Pretty fast for an older man,* Tice thought as he struggled to catch up. A waxing moon shed dim light on the ground as the two struggled to not trip over ruts and tree roots.

Soon they reached the edge of a field to the back of the rail station. Wakeman stopped at a big oak tree and held up a hand, signaling Tice to stand still. He peeked around the tree at the train station. Lanterns lit up the station dock and a small area around it. Steam from a train hissed as if the huge machine was anxious to get moving.

Wakeman pulled a watch from a pocket and held it toward the moonlight. "Nine fifty-nine," he said. "Train leaves in one minute and the station master thinks it's a sin to leave late. Hurry, son! But stay out of the light. I'll lift you on a boxcar near the back."

With that he took off, Tice on his heels. They ran along a treeline, with about fifty yards of field between the woods and the railroad tracks. The train stretched back from the station, its boxcars becoming increasingly vague and darker silhouettes.

Tice had to concentrate too hard on where he was running to look toward the station. If he had snuck a peak, he might have caught a glimpse of Morgan. The big man was stalking back and forth on the dock, twisting his mustache and grumbling, sometimes pounding the butt of his whip into the palm of his hand. The station building itself blocked Morgan's view of the woods except at the very end of the dock where, if he looked very closely, he might have noticed movement in the moonlight out in the field to the south.

Suddenly the train whistle blew twice and the wheels began to move, ever so slowly. Kaa—ching. *Oh, no!* Tice thought. *It's leavin' without me!*

Kaa—ching.

"Cross over, son," Wakeman called over his shoulder and turned to sprint across the field.

Ka-ching, ka-ching.

Tice pushed off in that direction but his toe caught on something, sending him sprawling. "Oomph!" he tumbled to the ground. The bundle containing his clothes and book fell out of one hand and the basket of food spilled out of the other.

Ka-ching, ka-ching, ka-ching. The train was slowly picking up speed, now reaching the speed of a fast walk.

Tice grabbed the bundle and reached for the basket. He saw the faint outline of a loaf of bread and an apple that had rolled out and he debated quickly if he had the time to pick them up.

"Hurry, son!" Wakeman urged from a few yards ahead.

Ka-ching, ka-ching, ka-ching, ka-ching..

The train was moving at fast jog speed. Three or four passenger cars were up front; the rest were boxcars.

"Tice! Hurry!" Wakeman was near frantic.

Finally Tice gathered the bundle and basket to his chest, got his legs moving and hurtled forward. But he could tell he was moving perpendicular to the rails and the train was moving forward. Could he make it?

Whoo-whoo! The steam engine's whistle was a sign the train was on its way.

Ka-ching, ka-ching morphed into clickity-clack.

Catching up to the clearly winded Wakeman, Tice reached the railroad bank, which was raised slightly above the field.

"This next boxcar!" Wakeman called loudly against the noise of the train on the tracks. "Toss your things in and push off my hands to jump aboard. You'll be met at the station at Newton, Massachusetts. Don't leave this boxcar!"

As the next boxcar approached, Tice readied to toss in his things. First the bundle, next the basket of food, and he raised his right foot into a stirrup Wakeman made with his two hands. With a mighty heave, Wakeman lifted Tice into the boxcar, which was rushing forward at a good pace now. Tice scraped his right knee on the opening to the boxcar, drawing blood, and he winced in pain.

As he grabbed his knee, the boxcar Tice was in approached the station dock.

Suddenly a dog's bark pierced the air, battling for dominance with the sounds of the train. Sitting on his buttocks, Tice peered forward out the door. Morgan and another man were on the dock! Morgan! And a big dog, a German shepherd, was looking square at his boxcar and barking! Angry barking!

Tice pushed himself backwards from the door, seeking the darkest part of the boxcar, hoping to become undetectable.

Oh, Lord, hide me! Hide me again!

The train was moving quickly now. Morgan and another man stared hard into each boxcar. *Did he see me?* Suddenly Morgan let the dog loose.

Oh, Lord! The dawg! Tice prayed into the darkness around him.

His teeth bared, the dog raced along the dock toward the train.

He does *see me, Lord! He's gonna jump in here and rip!*

The dog was gaining on the boxcar with each bound.

Hurry, train. Hurry!

The dog was so close Tice could see drool hanging at the corner of its mouth. *Please hurry!*

Suddenly, the big shepherd reached the end of the dock just as the boxcar swept past and he sprung toward the open door. Tice clenched his teeth, pushed his neck down between his shoulders and squeezed his eyes tight.

He didn't see what happened next, but he heard. The sound was a squeal, followed by a high-pitched yelp. Tice guessed the dog had missed the doorway, fell to the rails and was run over by the train wheels.

Poor dawg. Tice cringed, not even thinking how he had feared the dog just seconds before.

•••••

"Halt that train!" Morgan hollered, running back to the ticket office. "Halt that train!"

"Sorry, mister," came the reply from the scrawny little man under the green visor. "No stoppin' that train now and," he looked at his watch, "it's right on time, the way we like it here. Never been late; not goin' to start now."

"I think there's a stowaway on board!"

"Then a stowaway he'll be. Or is it a she?"

"He, she, what does it matter? You've gotta stop it!"

"Sorry," the man said and turned his attention to a book, ignoring the horse whip that Morgan held halfway to his shoulder with a fierce grip.

Fifty yards away to the south, Wakeman hurried back toward the woods.

•••••

A quarter mile to the north, Tice hunkered into a corner, having pulled his bundle and basket to his side.

"Thank You, Lord," he said aloud. "That was a close 'un. I didn't know Morgan was still on my trail." The thought of Morgan made him shiver. *'N a dawg, too. A big, snarly dawg droolin' for blood.*

Clickity-clickity-clackity-clack, clickity-clickity-clackity-clack. Each clickity meant more distance between him and Morgan, he thought. He smiled and looked up into the darkness. "You sure knows how to scares a chil'. Makes me call out to You more."

•••••

Tice was finally beginning to doze off and the sky

to the east was starting to lighten when, out of the dark a figure leaped up and through the open boxcar door. Tice stifled a scream and his heart leaped. All he could tell was that it was a tall, slim figure. It couldn't be Morgan. The person bent down on one knee.

"You here?" It was a young man's voice but high-pitched, like he was either scared or his voice hadn't fully changed yet.

Tice huddled in the front corner of the boxcar and figured the person's eyes hadn't yet adjusted to the darkness and they couldn't see him. He waited quietly.

"You here, Tice?"

Tice! he thought. Phew! He knows my name.

Tice drew a breath. "Yeah, right here," he whispered.

The figure nearly bounded to him, like the Jack-in-the-box Tice had seen Massah's young daughter playin' with.

"I'm Bob," the person said. "You're in Massachusetts. The train's about to come into Newton station. Follow me. We've got to jump off."

"Jump?" The thought scared Tice.

"Yes, jump. Don't worry. It's simple. 'sides, I know just where there's a hayfield and someone has just so happened to be kind enough to leave a big ole pile of hay right near the rail tracks. Ready?"

Tice certainly was not ready. But he didn't have time to object.

"Get your belongings if you have any, and let's go."

Tice grabbed for his things.

Bob had already leaped to the boxcar door. Does he ever simply walk? Tice wondered. Boy, he had met all types on this journey.

"Hurry!" Bob said. "Quick, quick!"

Clutching his belongings, Tice crawled up beside Bob and, without warning, Bob yanked him forward, out of the boxcar. A second later Tice landed, but softly like on a big soft cloud in the sky, his stuff falling on either side of him. Tice heard Bob land nearby, then felt something scratchy on his neck. And he smelled that wonderful, indescribable odor of newly cut hay. They'd made a perfectly timed landing into the hay pile Bob had mentioned.

"Ha-ha!" Bob laughed. "'Nother perfect fly into the night."

"You done this before?" Tice asked, looking at the hazy ghost of a figure.

"Sure. A dozen times 'n never missed this here haystack. C'mon, Tice."

"How d'ya' know my name?"

"Never mind. I jus' do."

Bob leaped to his feet and reached a hand down to help Tice up, then grabbed the daypack with his clothes and book, leaving Tice with his bag of food. "Follow me. Gotta get ya' where we're goin' 'fore the sun rises."

With that, Bob sprinted across the pasture. Tice hustled to keep up, looking in the dim light to see if the boy's feet ever touched the ground. Maybe not.

Their destination was the homestead of the widow Mary and three daughters of William Jackson. Tice spent most of the one day he was at the Jackson place hidden in the attic. Ellen Jackson, the prettiest young lady Tice had ever seen and with the curliest dark hair he ever laid eyes on, took special care to see he was well fed.

In the late afternoon she arrived with a plate filled with chicken, potato and spinach. She sat with him, telling him stories about her family, especially her father who had been a leading abolitionist against slavery when he died five years earlier, in 1855.

"Daddy started and owned a soap and candle

factory here in Newton," Ellen said, her eyes wet and her shoulders square but with not even a hint of pride. "He was a member of the Massachusetts General Court way before I was born and then served in the United States Congress. He even started our church, the Eliot Church, and headed the Temperance Society.

"But most of all," Ellen's eyes glistened, "he was a soldier for God. And, just like Uncle Francis, Daddy's fight was to free slaves."

Tice's face lit up with a smile. "That's me."

"Yes, Tice, but no longer. You're going north to Canada, where you will be a free man. And because you're heading north it gets colder. So Mother and her sewing-bee friends have made warm clothes for you."

Ellen held up a cloth bag beside her. "There's pants and a shirt and a sweater in here."

She handed the bag to Tice and he pulled out what he thought were surely the nicest-looking clothes he would ever wear—better even than those from Miss Jayne or the Randolphs—the nicest clothes from the prettiest girl.

As Tice admired his new garments Ellen told him how her father would argue against the yoke of slavery.

"Oh, Daddy, he'd attack the idea of slavery as fiercely as he'd defend the goal of freedom. He'd say to the pro-slavery people"—Ellen puffed up her chest and spoke in the deepest voice she could muster, making Tice laugh—'slavery is at war with virtue, with righteousness, and with God Himself.' He'd ask them, 'Do you want to be at war with God?'"

She shook her head, "Oh, Daddy. These people, Tice, they'd defend slavery by mentioning that it's in the Bible. But Daddy would inform them that slaves in the Bible weren't treated like you folks in the fields today. My, oh my, Joshua was a slave in Egypt but

Pharaoh put him in charge of the whole country!

"Daniel was a slave but King Nebuchadnezzar put him and his three friends in control of entire territories of his kingdom. When Father Abraham wanted a wife for his son Isaac, he sent out his head slave to find the right woman. Do you think that sounds like the slavery of today?"

Tice shook his head. Ellen smiled and took his hand in hers. "Nor do I."

•••••

That night a smile remained on Tice's face as he slept between two chimney supports that were covered with boards and racks of vegetables.

But again it was a sleep cut short. He found himself being hurried downstairs, his backpack now bulging with clothing. He followed Ellen and Mrs. Jackson along the hallway, down the stairway and toward the back of the house. As they hurried through the parlor Tice took time to notice a portrait that was dimly lit by a single candle in the room. It hung above a fireplace. Must be Misser Jackson, Tice thought, noticing the man's kind faced framed by a balding head and close-cropped beard. The man looked down on Tice with love in his eyes.

"Thank you, sir, for havin' such a nice fam'ly," Tice said softly, noticing that those eyes followed him as he passed by.

At the back door, Ellen turned to Tice. "Daddy'd say, 'We're sending you on to the Promised Land,' just like the Hebrews in the Bible." She smiled and hugged Tice.

"Tice," Mrs. Jackson said, "Bob here will take you on to your next connection, and they will transport you to Concord. God be with you, young man."

Tice looked out the door and saw Bob standing outside, behind the big Federalist house. "Hey," Tice said, waving to Bob.

"Hey, yourself. Come on, Tice, let's make hay. Ha! Get it?"

Tice didn't get it, but he dashed out the door, taking a quick glance at the Jackson ladies. "Thank you."

•••••

Bob glided along briskly, Tice at his elbow. They crossed a field, lit only by a half moon straight up above. When they entered a wood, Bob stooped and picked up a lantern that had been laid beside a big tree. He took three steps into the woods, removed the glass from the lantern, then lit a match and put it to the wick before returning the glass. He carefully heightened the flame just barely enough to light a few feet in front of them.

Apparently satisfied, Bob turned to Tice.

"I'll take one of your satchels," he said, reaching out his spare hand.

"Thanks." Tice handed him the lighter sack, which now carried a fresh loaf of bread, some cheese and two oranges from the Jacksons.

Fifteen minutes later they reached the end of the forest trail, which led into a small field. Bob turned off the lantern and set it down carefully. He pointed across the field to a large barn.

"Mister Barnes'll be waitin'." A minute later they were at the side of the barn and Bob opened a narrow door. Inside, a sturdy-looking, middle-aged man wearing a big hat and what appeared to be a long coat was tightening the bridle on an even sturdier-looking horse. He turned to look at the boys.

"Young man," he motioned to Tice, "let's put your

things in my saddlebag, then you can climb up behind me on this fine Morgan stallion and we'll be off. The mention of the name "Morgan" made Tice flinch. He could almost feel the whip.

There was time for only a short goodbye with Bob. A minute later Tice and Barnes were out of the door and on the hard-packed dirt road. Many hours later, as night ascended into sunrise and with Tice's fanny sore as all get-out, they arrived in Concord. Obviously avoiding the main street, Barnes rode the horse right up behind a large, two-story home.

Barnes turned to look over his shoulder at Tice. "We have to still be careful. Prying eyes."

"Prying eyes?" Tice had not heard this expression.

"People want to pry open any secrets. *You* are my secret, Tice. Let's keep you under wraps, okay?"

"Under wraps?"

Weary from travel, Barnes turned sharply to stare at Tice. Then his features relaxed and he replied, "Under wraps? Why, Tice, that means we want you to be like the wonderful gift people unwrap at Christmas time. You don't know what's under the wrapping until it's just the right time to open it. Do you understand?"

Tice's face lit up like a Christmas tree with a dozen candles hanging on its limbs.

Just then, the back door to the house opened and out stepped a short, bald and very nicely dressed man with thick eyeglasses. "Nathan," he called, "come in, come in. Leave your horse for my son."

The man stuck his head inside the door and beckoned, "Joel, come and bed down Mister Barnes's horse, will you? Grain him and put him in the rear stall by the tack room."

Barnes and Tice both dismounted. Barnes removed the saddlebag, hefted it over one shoulder and followed the man inside the house with Tice close behind.

A boy twelve or thirteen years old rushed past them, with a "Hello, sir" spoken toward Barnes and a nod to Tice, then disappeared outside.

Barnes set down the saddlebag and extended a hand. "Jonathan."

Jonathan Ball shook Barnes's hand, and looked toward Tice.

"Our newest ward, eh?"

"Too short a time to make him a ward, I'm afraid. We think there's a slave hunter close on his heels, so we're trying to rush him on as fast as possible," Barnes said.

"Yes-sir," Tice offered, "I saw him—Morgan, that is—at the railroad station back there in Con'cut."

"Norwich, Connecticut?"

"Yep. That's the place. Only he had a dawg. Never seen him with a dawg before. But I think the dawg's hurt—maybe dead."

"When was that, son?"

"Couple days ago."

"Only two days?"

"I's all night on the train. Then Bob tossed me overboard onto a hay pile, then I slept a couple hours 'n Misser Barnes tossed me onboard his hoss. Now I's here."

"Well, that sounds like a lot of tossing and not much sleep," Ball said. "Let's get you some rest, then we'll put you on a wagon to New Hampshire."

Tice smiled broadly although he had no idea where this "New Hampshire" was. The thought of sleep encouraged him. Not to mention getting off his fanny for a while.

A lady entered the room which, as Tice looked around he noticed, was a sort of anteroom off the main rooms of the house.

"Nathan!" the lady said and moved across the room

to offer him a hug.

"Mildred." Barnes returned the embrace.

"Mildred," Ball said, "do you suppose Margaret could put something together for our guests?"

"Of course. I'll see to it."

A few minutes later Tice and Barnes were eating bacon, sausage and eggs with thick homemade bread, covered with butter, and mugs of hot cocoa.

"This is a very fine house," Tice said to Barnes.

"Sure is. Mister Ball is a very fine goldsmith, famous for his work."

"Goalsmith?"

"Gold with a 'd.' He works with gold and creates beautiful jewelry and such."

"Wow."

"You might say that," Barnes smiled.

•••••

That night Barnes slept in a guest room while Ball escort-ed Tice to a hiding place around a beam and paneled chimney. It was small but a thick mattress filled the place. Tice lay down and a moment later, just as he was nodding off to a deep sleep, thought to himself that it felt like he was floating on a cloud—the softest cloud in God's universe.

Before daylight Jonathan Ball roused Tice.

"Sorry, but we have to get on the road."

With scrambled eggs, potatoes and a muffin in their stomachs, before sunrise, Ball and Tice said farewell to Mildred Ball and Nathan Barnes, who was returning home to Newton.

"One stop on the way," Ball said as he snapped the reins to the two horses pulling the wagon. Tice again was settled in the back of a wagon bed, readying himself to weather another day of bumpy roads.

A few minutes later the wagon stopped at a little house and Tice noticed the silhouette of a person quickstep down a walkway to the wagon, then climb aboard.

"This reminds me of staying up through the night at Walden to watch the birds at first light, Jonathan," the person said in a low voice.

Ball stifled a laugh. "Yeah, Judge. We want to set someone free as a bird." He pointed behind him. "Say hello to Tice."

The man looked back at Tice and extended a hand. "Name's Henry," he said.

"Hello," Tice said. "You a judge?"

The man winced.

"No," Ball said. "We call him Judge because he's so quiet and solemn all the time—though you'd never know it by his writings. Here's my challenge to you, young man: get Mister Thoreau here to laugh and I'll give you that whole bag of apples back there." He pointed to the corner of the wagon bed where a cloth bag stood.

"Are we off to West Fitchburg?" Thoreau asked.

"Not this time. Andover, here we come."

"To Bill Jenkins'?"

"Correct, mister nature man."

"I'll give you a dollar if you can even find the Jenkins place," Thoreau laughed.

"Make it two and it's a bet."

"Two it is. And I'll give you a hint: it's actually in *South* Andover."

Ball shook his head and feigned disgust. "I knew that."

The men shook hands.

Riding through woods and fields, Ball turned to Tice. "Mister Thoreau here is a famous writer—and a transcendentalist."

"Tran-send-alist?"

"I believe," Thoreau said, "there are things that are beyond what we can see or feel or smell."

"Oh. God!" Tice said.

Thoreau smiled. "You might say. I call him that."

"Good, 'cause that's what He calls Hisself." Tice grinned, glad that he could exchange words with this obviously grand man.

Ball clicked his tongue, snapped the reins and the horses took off at a goodly gait.

Thoreau turned to Tice. "Truly," he said, "our friend here overstates my connection to transcendentalism. Some call me a naturalist because I spend so much time out in nature. But they misunderstand the term 'naturalist.' Naturalists believe that the physical universe is all there is. That there's nothing beyond it. That's nowhere near what I believe.

"Others call me a transcendentalist, maybe because one of my best friends is Ralph Emerson. He thinks God and the universe are inseparable; they're one and the same. That God is an impersonal force or spirit behind the created world.

"Well, I say, 'Maybe.'"

Tice listened carefully but offered no comment.

Thoreau continued: "In the view of transcendentalism a person's ideal goal should be to grow beyond his individual self and 'become one' with ultimate reality. But as long as a person sees himself as an individual he will live selfishly and, therefore, will be doomed to reincarnation."

"Re-in—" Tice stumbled over the word.

"After you die, you're born again as another living creature."

"Yeah?" Tice said.

"Yes. Well so they *think*."

Tice laughed. "Then maybe I just ate Aunt Isabelle

yesterday when I ate that chicken?"

Thoreau began to laugh, then cut it short and settled back on the buckboard seat, mulling Tice's comment. "Hm-m-m."

As Tice rode along in the back of the buckboard behind Henry David Thoreau and Jonathan Ball Thoreau noticed the corner of the leather-bound *The Pilgrim's Progress* sticking out of Tice's daypack. He looked at Tice and reached hesitantly for the book. "May I?"

"Sure."

Thoreau felt the soft cover and turned it over in his hands. He eyed Tice and asked, "You read?"

"I'm learnin'. People are teachin' me. Maisey gave me that."

"Hm-m. And what do you know of God, young man?"

Tice shrugged his shoulders. "Jus' that He is."

"He is what?"

"He is—there."

"There?"

"Yeah. There. Everywhere. He's here."

"Here?"

"All 'round us."

"And you know this to be true?"

"Yeah."

"How do you know?"

"Well, He helps me. Every day."

"Uh-huh."

"He helped me 'scape from the plantashun."

"Uh-huh. How?"

"I never swum in my life, but I swum that day. All across the Ohio River." Tice hesitated, recalling the fright that turned to calm. "'N that river was flowin' somethin' fierce, too."

Interested, Thoreau leaned in toward Tice. "Go on."

"'N God led me to a lady's house who protected me from my Massah. Then He hid me, hid me good. 'N He hid me all the way up here t'where I am's now."

"But it was good people, not God, hiding you."

"Yeah and most all of 'em mentioned God speakin' to 'em, God leadin' 'em, God doin' this 'n that. So's I think they's all believe."

"Does believing make it so?"

"It makes it so to me."

Thoreau slowly nodded his head a couple of times, then turned to watch where they were riding. Ball remained silent, keeping his eyes on the road. It was tree-lined and not particularly wide.

A few more minutes passed and Thoreau again turned toward Tice.

"Here's my thought, Tice: People (maybe not you) believe truth to be remote, behind the farthest star." Thoreau pointed heavenward where faint lights still sprinkled the sky. "In eternity there is indeed something true and sublime. But all these times and places and happenings are here and now. God Himself culminates in the present moment."

Tice looked blankly at Thoreau through the dim pre-sunset.

"My neighbors," Thoreau went on, "tell me of their meeting famous gentlemen and ladies at the dinner table. But I care less of such things and I don't give a fig what's in the newspaper. What do these people talk about? Clothing. Manners. Posh! Dress it as you will, a goose is a goose.

"But my delight is not to walk hand-in-hand with this or that famous person but to walk in the here and now with the Builder of the universe, that Builder being God. What are men celebrating? They're all on a committee of arrangements, and hourly expect a speech from somebody. God is only the president of the day—

that's the here-and-now day, not the afar-off-in-eternity day. And every work I do, every pencil I make, every survey I complete, my only help is God and Him only."

Tice could understand this last bit but held his tongue.

Thoreau appeared to take the silence as a cue to continue. "Whereas transcendentalists believe truth and happiness can be found through intuition, human feelings and spirit, I really don't. I think people, at their core, are generally evil, sinful beings."

Tice thought of Lykins and Morgan and nodded his head. Then he thought of Miss Jayne and Alden and Alden Randolph and Bobby and Nathan Barnes. They weren't evil, were they? Mandy Randolph even began teaching him how to read and she used the Bible to do it.

"So," Thoreau asked, "are you a Christian?"

"Yes-sir."

"This is my thought of Christians, Tice. Tell me if this describes you."

"Yes-sir."

"The modern Christian man consents to say all the prayers in the worship book, provided you'll let him go straight to bed and sleep quiet afterward."

"I don't know 'bout worship books but I pray to God all times of the day, Misser Thoreau."

"Uh-ha. Well, I think all these Christians' prayers begin with 'Now I lay me down to sleep,' and he's forever looking forward to the time when he'll go to his long rest in heaven."

"I don't know 'bout layin' down t' sleep but I do look forward t' goin' t' heaven and seein' my Pappy and my Mamma."

"A-ha." Thoreau thought for a moment. "The Christians I'm talking about have consented to perform certain old-established charities—that's helping others—but do not wish to hear of any new-fangled ones. They don't wish to have any supplementary articles, so to speak, added to the contract, to fit it to the present time."

"Well, sir, I don't know 'bout helpin' others or not. It seems that's what God wants us t' do, not *not* do. He says, 'Love others as we love us-uns ourselves.' Right?"

Thoreau nodded. "True. That's what the Bible says."

"Then that's what *He* says." Tice knew that, for sure.

"The Christian I'm speaking about, Tice, shows the whites of his eyes on Sunday but the blacks all the rest of the week. The evil is not merely a stagnation of blood, but a stagnation of spirit as well."

"That sounds like Massah to me."

"Who?"

"My Massah who owns the plantashun."

"He goes to church on the Sabbath?"

"Uh-huh."

"Then rides herd over you the rest of the week?"

"Uh-huh."

"Well, he's the Christian I'm talking about."

"He ain't no Christian t'll, sir. My Pappy said goin' t' church don't make you no Christian any more 'n me workin' in a cotton field makes me a ball 'o cotton."

Thoreau sat back straight and laughed. He put his hand to his mouth and looked at Ball. "Where'd you get this young man, Jonathan?"

Ball chuckled. "Met your match?"

"Match? Lucky it's not chess."

•••••

A few more minutes passed, then Thoreau turned

once more to Tice.

"One thing I know," he said, "no man was meant to be slave to another. Therefore, this Fugitive Slave Act calls out to all right-thinking people to be disobeyed. It's crucial, appropriate and even urgent to disobey such an unjust creature."

Miss Jayne had told Tice about the Fugitive Slave Act, the federal law that sought to force the authorities in northern, or free states to return fugitive slaves to their masters. The law empowered police officers and watchmen to act as what abolitionists considered kidnappers and slave catchers.

Ball elbowed Thoreau. "We're approaching *South* Andover, my friend. You're going to owe me that two-bit bet."

Thoreau turned to look where the wagon was headed. "Yep, you're right, Jonathan. I was just going to tell our young friend here what I've told you before: It's that government, the same one that enacted the Fugitive Slave Act, is best which governs least."

"Laissez-faire," Ball said.

"Laissez-faire. Yes. The government—our government, any government—should stay out of everyday personal affairs. And I'll add this—having been behind bars myself: Under a government which imprisons any unjustly, the true place for a just man is also a prison."

"You volunteering to return there?"

Thoreau chuckled.

A few minutes later, as the sky was lightening over the eastern horizon, they turned off the road and settled beside a large brown house.

A very short, very squat man with very long arms hustled out of the house, motioning them to follow him.

"This way. This way," he said as he trotted to a small barn and opened the double-door wide for the wagon. "The forest here-abouts is thick, but prying eyes are everywhere."

Once inside, Jonathan Ball said, "We can't stay, Bill."

"Breakfast with Hildy and me and be gone, then. But breakfast with us, first."

There was no turning the invitation aside and, minutes later, there was no turning aside bacon, scrambled eggs, wedges of potato, sliced tomato, a small mountain of toast and thick milk such as Tice had never before tasted as Hildy Jenkins single-handedly served up a feast.

Chewing on cottage bacon, Thoreau looked directly at Tice. Once inside the house Tice had his first chance to actually see the man who had been his companion from Newton to South Andover. Thoreau had a long thin nose, a thin face, thin chin, wide-set eyes, straight brown hair down over the top of his ears and wispy whiskers along and below his chin line. Nothin' much unusual on the outside to reveal the smarts inside, Tice thought.

"You have a new life ahead of you, Tice," Thoreau said, "and I hope you seek the right things in it. People will encourage you to seek riches. Don't be overly influenced by them. And don't be discouraged no matter what poverty you might confront. The sunset is reflected from the windows of a hut as brightly as from those of a castle, and the snow melts before its door as early in the spring. The fault-finder will find faults even in paradise. Love your life, rich as it is or poor as it may be. Find your life in the living of it."

"Find my life in the livin' of it," Tice repeated, contemplating the words.

"You know," Thoreau said, "most people have not delved six feet beneath the ground, nor leaped as many feet above it. We know not where we are. Besides, we're sound asleep nearly half our time."

Tice nodded, thinking about the mention of six feet up and six feet down and thought of "up" being toward Heaven and "down" being toward that other place Pappy warned him about.

Thoreau continued: "Recently I stood over an insect crawling amid the pine needles on the forest floor and endeavoring to conceal itself from my sight. I asked myself why it hid its head from me who might, perhaps, be its helper. And as I stood there I was reminded of the greater Benefactor and Intelligence that stands over me the human insect.

"Don't hide yourself from Him, Tice. He may indeed have great treasures of wealth, but He may have even greater wealth of the treasures of ingenuity, innovation, inner conscience, the ability to discover who you are inside."

"No, sir," Tice said. "I don't hide myself from the Lord 'n I won't."

Thoreau patted Tice on the arm. "Good man. Tice, the sincerity I see in you is in such short supply in this world. Do I see it in my rich neighbor's face? In the church deacon's countenance? In the postmaster's, or carpenter's, or ferrier's visages? No, but right here before me—in the smiling, inquisitive expression of a young slave. I'm sincerely glad I met you."

"We ought to be on the road," Bill Jenkins interrupted as he laid a napkin on the table. "Gotta get this free man north to Maine and through to New Brunswick."

"Tice," Thoreau said, "never will you meet a better people than those of Maine, especially the Indians. One of my best friends is an Indian in Maine—Joe Polis, who lives in Old Town. Like Joe, if you befriend them, they'll be a friend to you. Everywhere you go, people may be obliged to help you, but they will not be obligated. Always, always be aware of the calm, for danger can meet you at that very spot. It's happened to me—not in ways that you may fear but in ways of nature when you paddle a canoe on the glassiest of waters then find quite a sea running, with waves that can fill your lap."

"Beware," Tice affirmed.

"Yes, beware."

"Yes-sir. Thank you, sir."

"I hope you'll think of me and Mister Ball and Mister and Misses Jenkins here as friends, not as sirs and madams," Thoreau said.

Tice offered his broadest, most winning smile and nodded assent.

Chapter Five
Onward Toward Canada

Tice thought of the three months that had passed since he and Alden Randolph rode into Jonathan Conrad's barn. From white family to white family, he was taken northeast, further and further away from the only "home" he knew, the plantation. Further and further from his friends; that made him sad. And further and further from Master; that made him glad. But not further and further from Morgan; that sent chills along his spine. Could this leg of this non-stop race leave Morgan far enough behind that he'd never catch up?

Most of the travel had been by wagon. Once a fine lady hid him in the luggage compartment in back of her carriage.

"Portland, that's where we're headin'," said Donald. In three short days Tice had come to love this boy almost like a brother. Donald kidded with him. Donald teased him. Donald taught Tice to read even better than Mindy Randolph and the others had along the way. Donald talked to him about Donald's problems and listened when Tice talked about his own. They talked about life, about death, about girls, about having families some day, about slavery, about freedom. All in all, Donald treated Tice same as himself. Same as Donald's real brother, Sammy.

"Portland," Tice repeated. "What's it like?"

"It's the biggest city I've been to. But I ain't been to Boston, which is loads bigger."

"Will you stay with me awhile?"

Donald hesitated, then replied, "Naw. Can't. Gotta get back home."

"Where we goin'?"

"I'm not supposed to tell ya', Tice."

Tice was perplexed. "Why not?"

"Causin' if you're caught the authorities might be able to beat the names outta ya'."

Tice flinched. Again the thought of the strands of a whip flashed through his mind.

"And you heard Dad say last night that the man lookin' for you was makin' noise back in Portsmouth."

Tice nodded his head.

"Well, you remember Portsmouth's not that far away."

Tice nodded again.

"Well, we've gotta go to Portland 'cause that's the next stop in the network, the Underground Railroad they're callin' it. But that's probably where that man'll be lookin', too."

Tentacles of fear ran up Tice's back like a swarm of little snakes. He shivered. "He's that close, huh?"

"That close," Donald answered firmly, holding a hand up with thumb and forefinger less than an inch apart.

A few minutes later as they came upon a river, Donald asked, "You hungry?"

"Yup."

"Then let's pull over there and picnic." Donald pointed to a large oak tree hugging the bank of the Kennebunk River about twenty yards away, then reined the horse in that direction.

"What's 'picnic'?"

"Sit down on the ground, lean back up against that big elm tree and chow down," Donald explained, pointing.

"Chow down?"

"Eat!" Donald explained, sounding exasperated. "Sorry, Tice. Didn't mean to yell. There's words 'n stuff you couldn't have learned livin' on that plantation and workin' in the fields. Picnicking is just takin' your time and enjoyin' your food and maybe fishin' a bit. But, heck, I brought no pole to fish with."

"I couldn't do it anyhow," Tice said.

"Sure you could. As good as me. I'd like to show you some day."

Donald pulled his horse Pop off the road and tethered him to a bush; they both dismounted and pulled off the saddlebag. A few minutes later, they were leaning back against the big old oak tree eating sandwiches of bread and beef and chewing on carrots.

"You'll be safe once I can get you to Portland and they can move you *out* of Portland," Donald said. "The anti-slavery movement is strong there. My Dad told me about a runaway slave who stowed himself aboard the Albion Cooper, a British brig loaded with lumber from Savannah, Georgia, just three years ago, in 1857. The captain discovered the stowaway and promptly consulted Samuel Waterhouse, who owns a clothing store on Fore Street. That night, Mister Waterhouse and a group of other anti-slavery folks and black men boarded the brig and rescued the runaway. By morning he was on his way to Canada."

"Can-da!" Tice said. "Freedom-Land."

Donald smiled but held up an index finger. Tice knew this meant directions—or a warning—were coming. "Yes, Tice, the anti-slavery movement is strong in Portland, but the slave catchers aren't no dumbies. Nope, they're not. And the thought of this Morgan guy makes me nervous. The way you speak of him, he's one mean fellow—cruel and ruthless, and with a base tongue to boot."

Tice nodded agreement. "Yep. All that."

"Hey, let's talk 'bout something more cheerful," Donald said. Watching at the river flowing by, his eyes widened and he looked back at Tice, he said, "We can't fish but, hey, see those twigs blown into the river?"

Tice peered down the riverbank. "Yeah."

"I'll betcha which one beats the other downstream."

"Okay."

"I'm bettin' on the one that isn't dead, that has the green leaves on it," said Donald.

"Then the other's mine, but I ain't got nothin' to bet," said Tice.

"Loser gets a punch on the arm."

"Okay."

The boys shook hands and started rooting on their twigs.

"Go, Speedy, go!" said Tice.

"Speedy?" Donald looked at Tice and chuckled.

"Speedy," Tice affirmed.

Donald turned his eyes toward the river. "Go faster ah-h—go even speedier, Swift."

"Swift?" Tice returned the grin.

"Don't pick on mine's name 'n I won't pick on yours."

"Agreed. Go, Speedy!"

"Go, Swift!"

"Go, Speedy!"

"Go, Swift!"

"Speedier, Speedy!"

"Swiftier, Swift!"

The boys started rolling on the grass, clutching at

their ribs in pain they were laughing so hard.
Finally, Donald pulled himself up on his knees.
"Aw, gosh, Tice, you're funnier 'n—"
Suddenly Donald put his finger to his lips. "Sh-h-h," he whispered with intensity. But Tice giggled on, rolling down the embankment toward the river.
"Quiet," Donald insisted, then leaped toward Tice to grab his attention. Finally reading the uneasiness in his friend's eyes, Tice put a hand over his own mouth and lay still.
Donald put a finger on an earlobe, indicating for Tice to listen.
Voices came from nearby, over the sounds of horse hoofs on gravel.
"Listen, Morgan, if your boy's there, we'll find him. Find him and take him back to Lykins' plantation. And if my boy's there we'll take him back to Lakeport Plantation down in Kentucky Bend, where I expect a nice reward from one Mister Lycurgus Johnson."
"I'd like to skin the little rodent if I find 'im," Morgan said.
Lying on his stomach by the river, Tice bristled at the sound of the man he knew all too well. A sudden jolt of fear felt like it stopped his heart from beating.
"Skin 'im 'n you don't get no reward."
"Skin 'im 'n my reward's in the skinnin'."
"Your boss ain't my boss," the man replied. "As a bounty hunter, the reward money's my only pay. So leave my boy alive no matter what you want to do with yours, hear?"
"Oh, I hear ya'."
Suddenly Morgan sat straight up in his saddle and looked in the direction of the riverbank.
"Stoppy here, Nate."
"Wha—?"
Morgan held up his hand and motioned his comrade

to be quiet.

"Somethin' by the river."

Tice and Donald peered through tall grass at the two men as the one called Nate stopped his horse and looked in their direction. They both dropped their heads to the ground.

"Nothin'. Don't see nothin'," the Nate fellow said.

"I don't, neither. But I did. And there's a horse tied up over there." Tice looked up again, in time to see Morgan pointing at Donald's gelding.

Morgan wrapped the reins around the saddle horn and climbed off his horse. Untying a whip from the back of his saddle, he headed toward the river. Panic struck Tice and he slithered backwards toward some deeper grass.

"Now don't go messin' up some young lovers there, Morgan," the man teased.

Morgan chuckled. "Nothin' like that. Just checkin' it ain't someone else, someone we might want to have a talk with."

•••••

As Morgan neared an oversized elm tree, Donald walked up big-as-you-please from the riverbank.

"Hi-ya', sir," Donald said cheerily. "I was just down washin' my hands."

Morgan stared at Donald, his eyes narrowing. He glanced at the food beneath the tree, then looked back at Donald.

"Who's with ya'?"

"With me?"

"Yeah. You with a girlfriend, maybe?"

"No, sir. Just myself."

"And that's the truth, is it?"

Donald hesitated, then knew why the man asked the

question. *Two sandwiches! He saw the two sandwiches! Don't panic. Don't panic. What did Dad say about circumstances like this? Pray! That's it: pray. Okay, Lord, fill my mouth. Answer the question for me!*

Morgan brought his arm, the one holding the whip, around from behind his back, then crossed his arms—letting the lash of the whip fall to the ground.

Donald swallowed hard.

"Well?" the big man asked.

"No, sir. I was bringing a friend, but he ended up not being able to come. Had to help his dad fix a fence."

"So he's fixin' a fence, huh?"

"Yep." Donald felt his hands shaking and a tight knot in his throat. He stuffed his hands in his pockets to hide the fact he was scared as a field mouse being chased by a fox.

He wished his dad was there with him, but his dad had to travel to Lyn, Massachusetts, to cover a New England Methodist Conference. Donald was proud his dad was one-of-a-kind, but also wished he weren't, so that his dad would be in charge of this trek to freedom for Tice.

Donald had accompanied his dad with other runaways, so he knew his way. But he'd never really felt danger before. Danger was always an idea, some distant afterthought, not something he could feel or taste. But now he both felt and tasted it. He felt it down his spine, which tingled, and in his hands, which shook. And he could taste it in his mouth, something like copper, or tin maybe.

"And you decided not to help him but to go for a picnic alone," Morgan said.

"Yep." Now his left eye was twitching!

"Why the two sandwiches?" Morgan wasn't looking at Donald now, but surveying the immediate land around them. Donald followed Morgan's gaze. Some underbrush along the river. Tall grass along the immediate riverbank. Several large trees a few yards from the riverbank. It all looked all right, but Donald knew himself that it all felt like something was amiss.

Donald looked down at the sandwiches. "Well, my Mom made sandwiches for both my friend and me, but since he didn't come I got two."

"And you've taken a few bites out of each, I see."

"Well—yeah."

"Strange."

An odd tingle twitched at the corner of Donald's mouth. "I—I, eh, I didn't know which I'd like best, the beef or the chicken, so I ate some of each."

Morgan bent down on a knee to get a close look at the sandwiches, then looked Donald squarely in the eye. "And which did you like best?"

"The—the beef."

"Well, that's good, boy, since both sandwiches are beef."

Morgan rose and Donald took a step back.

"I'm surprised it ain't fish, boy, since your story's smells like it."

Morgan pounded his whip twice into his left palm, then pushed Donald aside and strode quickly toward the river.

Donald gulped, panicking. *Help, Lord! Hide Tice!*

Morgan reached the riverbank and scrutinized the tall grass and underbrush.

"What ya' got, Morgan?" The question came from Nate, who, after watching the verbal exchange, had dismounted his horse and walked to the elm tree.

"Not sure. Nothin' yet."

Nate walked up to Donald and took hold of his shoulders. "What you hidin', boy?"

Intimidated by the man's size and demeanor,

Donald had never been so afraid in his life, 'cept maybe that time he got his foot caught in the waterwheel which was turning lickity-split.

He tried to breath deeply to suck in oxygen that eluded his lungs, then blurted out, "Why, nothin', mister. I promise! I'm just here for a picnic."

"All alone?"

"All alone. My friend Billy was comin' but he can't. I thought I could bring my girlfriend, Nel, but she couldn't make up her mind. Silly thing. So I came alone."

"Nel, huh?"

"Well, maybe she's not my girlfriend, but she would be, if she were smart."

Nate chuckled. "If'n she were smart, eh?"

Donald forced a smile. *Where was Tice, anyhow? Hide good, Tice!*

Donald looked toward Morgan, who was walking very slowly along the riverbank toward the ocean a distance away. He was slapping that whip handle into his palm and Donald remembered what Tice had told him about Morgan and that whip. He shivered.

Maybe it was only a few seconds but it seemed an hour to Donald. Finally, Morgan stomped his way quickly back to Donald.

"Where you from, boy?" Morgan asked.

"Kennebunk," Donald lied.

"Last name?"

"Banks," he lied again.

"First name?"

"Donald."

"Donald Banks from Kennebunk, huh?"

Donald nodded.

"Your papa's name?"

"Henry."

"Henry Banks from Kennebunk."

Donald nodded again.

"I'll remember that, Donald. I will."

With that, Morgan walked quickly past Donald and motioned for Nate to follow him.

As he neared his horse, Morgan looked back at Donald and smiled crookedly. "Eat hearty, boy."

Donald nodded, tried to smile and, when Morgan turned away, exhaled. Stiffly, he watched the two men ride off northward, over the bridge and out of sight.

Then he wandered back to the riverbank and scanned the tall grass for signs of Tice. Not a trace. *That fella's disappeared! He could be a magic-show act.*

When he finally felt the danger had passed, he called out, "Hey, Tice. Come on out!"

Nothing happened—not a sound and no Tice. A minute passed. Two minutes.

Donald walked down to where he and Tice had lain on the riverbank and looked for a clue to where Tice had gone. He wondered if Tice had swum the river, like he did the Ohio, or simply run as far away as he could get so as Morgan couldn't find him. If so, Donald would never get Tice to Portland, never mind to Mariners' Church. A feeling of alarm started to overtake him. What if? What should he do? Go on to Portland, looking for Tice? Return home?

Again, Donald looked up and down the riverbank and then walked along, examining the area. No signs of anyone walking through the tall grass. No footprints on the mucky shoreline. Yes, indeed, Tice *had* disappeared. Puff!

Donald decided to return to the big elm tree and wait awhile longer, but before heading back he called out again, "Tice. Come on out, if'n you're there!"

Suddenly, Tice dropped from the tree directly in front of him. Right out of the branches above.

A big smile widened across Tice's face. "I can't fish, but I surely can climb a tree!"

Donald laughed and hugged his friend. "I thought you was off a-runnin'. Miles away, maybe. And I'd never see you ag'in."

"Sorry," Tice said, "but I wanted to make sure Morgan was really, truly, honest-to-God gone."

Donald wiped drops of sweat from his brow. "That's a scary man."

Tice nodded with exaggeration. "Uh-huh."

"That's a big whip."

"Uh-huh."

"And he's got the biggest hands."

"Uh-huh."

"And ugly dark eyes!"

"Uh-huh."

"And a big red nose!"

"Uh—" Tice caught himself. "Big red nose?"

Donald laughed and punched him on the shoulder. "Jus' wanted to see if you was listenin'."

Tice laughed and tackled him to the ground. The boys rolled down the riverbank, hooting and pushing at each other as they went. They finally stopped just short of the water.

•••••

The second day after their scare, Donald and Tice reached Portland. Donald steered Pop toward the docks along the tidal Fore River which flowed out into Casco Bay and the Atlantic Ocean beyond. Portland was a bustling city, with some ships sailing and a few steamers chugging in and out.

Donald and Tice looked about. Two-story houses, some with widows' walks and nearly all of them painted white, spread from the docks up a hill to a long ridge. The ridge ran parallel to the harbor and afforded a view of the ocean without and a large bay that circled around behind the town within. It was a pretty sight.

"That the osh-un?" Tice asked breathlessly.

"Near 'nough."

"Wow! The osh-un!"

Donald looked back over his shoulder at Tice and smiled.

"Yeah." Donald pointed to a dock about a half-mile in front of them. "That's where the Prince of Wales set sail from just a couple weeks ago."

"Prince a whales?"

"The King of England's son."

Tice nodded. "Uh-huh."

Donald smiled and bumped his pal with an elbow. "Never mind. Jus' 'nother guy—like you 'n me." He hesitated. "Only he's got barrels 'n barrels of money."

Tice chuckled. "You're kiddin' me again, Donald. No one hauls their money 'round in barrels—not even Massah."

"Your Massah's in the poor house compared to the Prince of Wales!" Donald turned and pointed a short distance to the left of the docks. "See that church spire up ahead?"

There was a church steeple here, another there and another further beyond as they looked eastward. "First Parish Church is up on the ridge. The Abyssinian Church is that one in the distance to the east. But—" Donald pointed his finger toward a smaller steeple down the hill from First Parish Church and near the docks.

"Uh-huh." Tice said. "I sees it."

"That's where we're headin'."

With that, Donald gave a nudge to Pop and off they rode. Rain had fallen overnight, creating puddles along the dirt streets and patches of mud here and there. Tice gazed around him. This place was much bigger than Maysville from where he had escaped, a lot smaller than Boston where he had passed through a couple weeks ago, and a lot prettier than both.

Just then a wagon splashed by in the opposite direction, its wheels kicking up mud that splattered his leg and the side of Pop. *Well, not **that** pretty.*

Several minutes passed. They rode along, Donald keeping the harbor to their right a couple of streets away. Tice watched the docks. Sail ships were anchored, their sails down, their tall masts sticking up like naked tree trunks toward the sky. Men bustled about, carting big boxes off the ships and toting others onboard. Some were hollering orders to others. Some were cussing at others.

It's like ants around an ant hill, Tice thought. Like us'uns on the plantashun when pickin' cotton. Only with a cool breeze from the osh-un. That sure would help on those hot days when the sweat's porin' down your neck.

Tice couldn't tell by the way they were dressed, who were the bosses and who weren't. Nothing like the plantation where Lykins and Morgan lorded it over everyone with whips in their hands, Morgan's hat turned a bit to one side and Lykins' face a full scowl much of the time.

"We're gettin' off here." Donald's voice cut into Tice's memories. Donald pulled Pop to the side of the street and Tice slid down to the ground while Donald tied the reins to a hitching post.

"Church's right around the corner and down the street here, then across the next one, Fore Street. We wanna be careful 'n on the lookout," Donald said.

"Uh-huh."

Donald took a saddlebag off the wagon and tossed it up onto his shoulder with a grunt. They might have eaten all the grub out of it, but it was still a big pack of leather for a teenager. It still contained Tice's daypack.

They walked past a hack stand where two men stood idly leaning on the wall outside, watching them curiously and causing Tice to look away, avoiding eye contact. Then they passed a livery barn where a huge bald man was banging on a horseshoe in the background while at street-side an obese, rich-looking man squabbled with the storeowner about a wagon wheel and, no, the problem with the wheel was not caused by his weight.

A sign by the doorway said it cost sixty cents to rent a horse-and-buggy rig for a couple of hours and $2.10 to use it for a day. Tice had no idea how much that was. He still had the money Alden had given him in his pocket, but it was a foreign substance to him, something to which he could not relate. Next was a tack store where a pretty teenage girl with her mother was cooing over a "simply exquisite lady's saddle, Momma."

Then they turned a corner and started walking downhill on a narrower, cobblestone side street. The docks were in sight in front of them.

Donald pointed ahead and to the left. "There, around that corner is Mariners' Church, Tice. We wanna walk carefully up to the building at the corner and peek 'round, make sure no one's there that shouldna' be before we step across the street to it."

"Uh-huh."

Donald gazed at Tice and said, "I wish you could stay with us, Tice, so's we could expand your vocab'lary a bit."

"Uh-huh." Suddenly Tice caught himself. As he stopped short, he was struck by the knowledge that he would soon say goodbye to the boy who had become his closest friend. He hung his head and shook it in dismay at the oddity of life. There were two worlds—slave and free—and he came from the wrong one. Why, God? he wondered.

Donald lowered his shoulder to drop the saddlebag on the ground and turned to face Tice.

"Tice, I got one brother, Sammy. But now you're my brother, too, okay?"

Tice nodded and his eyes welled up.

"I trust you like I'd trust my brother."

The tear began a trek down Tice's cheek.

"I'd do everythin' for ya' that I'd do for Sammy."

Tice nodded and swiped at the tear.

"And I know you'd do for me what a brother'd do."

"Sure would."

"So, brothers are never separated like forever, right?"

Tice shrugged.

"Never. Not here." Donald pointed to his heart.

Another tear appeared.

"'N you're my brother in Christ, too, right?"

Tice's face was a question mark.

"That means you believe in Jesus like I do. We're in His family. He saved us from our sins, right?"

Tice nodded and smiled.

"So we're brothers in two ways. Two ways!"

The tear had reached Tice's chin and a new one was heading downward now, too. He didn't even try to swipe them away.

"So that's two reasons we won't be apart—in here." Donald pointed to Tice's heart. "Okay?"

"Okay."

Donald chuckled. "See? We're expanding your vocab'lary already."

Tice smiled and finally did wipe a tear away.

"Okay," Donald said, then turned back. Tice watched as he stealthily approached the corner of the building, then peeked around it, and almost fell back into Tice's arms. There was fear on Donald's face, for sure.

"Morgan!" Donald whispered hoarsely.

Tice's eyes widened.

Donald nodded. "Morgan and that weird, scary guy travelin' with him—Nate."

Donald steadied himself and straightened up, then edged back to the corner as if a poisonous snake were coiled on the other side.

"Careful!" Tice whispered hoarsely.

Gingerly Donald edged his right eye to the last brick on the corner and stuck his head out ever so minutely, until he could again glimpse what was happening.

Donald turned to Tice and held up a hand. "Morgan and Nate are talkin' to Rev'rund Randall."

Inwardly, Tice had known the possibility existed that they would run into his adversary here in Portland, but he was still startled. "No!" came out of his mouth before he could slam his hand over it. Frightened, he turned and ran back up the hill and lurched into an alley between two buildings. A large barrel stood in the alley and Tice ran to hide behind it.

•••••

Donald nearly called to Tice to stop running up the street, but figured he should listen to the conversation in front of the church. Then he'd know what they were facing and could go and find Tice with a plan in hand. Again he peered around the corner of the building.

"—reputation for hidin' runaway slaves and that reputation don't stop here in Portland," Morgan growled. "We've heard about you as far away as Portsmouth."

"So don't go tryin' t' lie 'bout it, rev'rund," said Nate. "We're not the only slave hunters around. We could bring a crowd of 'em over here and do serious damage to this here buildin'."

"I'm well aware of the slave hunters," Reverend Randall replied. "First, there's a big difference between 'slave hunters' and 'slave catchers.' And second, you're not the first ones of either kind to threaten me and my church. But, no matter what people say, you'll discover that no slave has ever been found in my church, your threats notwithstanding—"

Reverend Randall pointed to the weapon in Morgan's hand, "and your whip notwithstanding, either."

Morgan snarled. "You'd better be prayin' that you 'n my whip never meet close-up, friend."

Reverend Randall did not flinch. "If you want to get the law to come back and look through my church, feel free to do so. Otherwise, please do not darken my door again, sir."

Nate, with menace in his eyes, took a step closer to Reverend Randall. But Morgan grabbed his elbow. "Let's check the docks, Nate."

Morgan looked at Reverend Randall. "We'll be keepin' an eye on you, mister. You 'n yours 'n this here church. Don't think we won't and don't think we can't do as I said 'n bring a mob of us slave *catchers* to take a close look, firsthand, under every floorboard and behind every wallboard in this here place."

With that, Morgan and Nate stalked off down the street and rounded the corner, heading to the docks just two blocks away. Hands on hips, Reverend Randall watched them disappear, then looked to the blue sky above, his lips moving with words unheard—by anyone on earth.

⋅⋅⋅⋅⋅

A minute later the two men had disappeared from sight and Donald sprinted back up the street to find Tice, calling his name. Two minutes later the two of them were running to the church and entering its doors.

"Reverend Randall!" Donald called. "Reverend Randall!"

The pastor stepped out of a door to the side of the pulpit. Seeing Donald and Tice, worry filled his face. "Come, come!" he called, waving them to him anxiously as he stepped back through the door.

Once the boys entered the back room, Donald introduced Tice. Reverend Randall smiled warmly. "Donald, we have to move swiftly," he said and turned to Tice. "Don't worry, young man, we'll get you to freedom, but two men are keen to capture you. They were just here minutes ago. We must get you to another station, and quickly."

Fear shook Tice's body.

Donald grabbed his hand. "Don't worry, Tice. Reverend Randall has the Lord on his side."

Tice nodded in agreement.

Reverend Randall spoke to Donald. "Do you know where Reuben Ruby's hack stand is?"

Donald shook his head. "Never heard of it."

"Then let me take that saddlebag for you and follow me."

Reverend Randall, a good half-foot taller than Tice, flung the saddlebag over his shoulder—maybe the tallest man Tice had ever seen. Leaving the church by a side door, he turned left and walked quickly up the hill, his long strides making the boys move quickly to keep up with him. When they got near the top of the ridge, the pastor looked over his shoulder, scanning the street below.

"Can't be too careful," he said. Then he turned left, walked another fifty yards along the street and crossed to the other side.

The sign "Reuben Ruby's Hack Services" stood over a wide barn-like door. Two carriages stood outside, both obviously newly painted black and well kept. A single horse was harnessed to each, the leather glistening with oil. An African-American man sat in the front one, reading a newspaper. The other was riderless.

Reverend Randall hurried between the two and waved the boys into the building.

Tice could feel the heat from a forge inside the barn. Red-hot embers sizzled as a heavy-set white man lifted a hammer and banged on a piece of iron, completely unaware of their presence.

"In here," Reverend Randall said and ushered the boys into a small side room. A handsome African-American man sitting behind a desk stood up when they entered. His eyes went from Reverend Randall to Donald and finally to Tice. Then a smile played at the corners of his mouth. He nodded at Tice and Tice immediately knew that this man knew him, his story, his race for life, his fear of being caught. Knew him.

"Boys, this is Mister Ruby," Reverend Randall said. "Reuben, this is Donald. This is Tice. A slave hunter from Tice's plantation is close on his heels; he and another man just stopped by our door looking for him."

"'N he almost caught him on the way here—back at Kennebunk River," Donald blurted out. "Only Tice hid up a tree."

Reuben laughed loudly and looked squarely at Tice with warm, chocolate-brown eyes. "You're going to have to continue to be good at hiding—until we can get you clear to Canada, son. But it looks like right now we'd better get you away from the waterfront."

His mouth agape, Tice gazed at Reuben.

Curious, Reuben asked, "What is it, son?"

"You's black," Tice declared.

"Thanks for pointing it out." Reuben laughed.

"If'n you're Mister Ruby than this is your biz-ness."

"That's true, son."

"You's black but you's not a slave 'n you own this biz-ness." It was a statement of fact, like Tice was repeating a lesson learned in school, trying to absorb the impact of the fact.

"True again, son."

"So people pay you 'n you pay 'ployees."

"Yes."

"You a runaway slave?"

"No, son." Reuben shook his head. "My daddy was a slave. Matter of fact, he was the best slave, a slave who his master learned to trust. Trusted him with a lot. Trusted him to run one of his farms. Then one day his master walked right up to my daddy and handed him a legal paper. Said he loved my daddy like a son. Said the paper declared him a free man."

Reuben's eyes started watering. "Then he gave my daddy what he called 'seed money.' Said it was like God's people planting seeds and setting people free. Told him to travel north away from slave country and plant the 'seed.' So he did, and here I am—a free man with a business."

"Wow!" Tice said. "Best thing my Massah ever gave me was a 'good goin', boy.'"

Reuben shook his head. "A better future lies ahead, son." Then he stepped to the door, opened it and called out, "Alysius!"

A short, thin, older African-American man wearing nicely ironed pants, a white shirt with bowtie and sporting a goatee stepped out of nowhere. "Yes-sir."

"Slave hunters are after this young man. Get him to the Fessenden place—now."

"Yes-sir." Alysius nodded his head, took measure of Tice, then motioned to him. "This way, young fella."

Tice hesitated and looked at Donald.

"Go on, Tice," Donald said. "Hide well, my brother."

The world was spinning around Tice. Was this real? Was this happening to him, or was it a dream? How could it be real? All these people helping him? Him!?

"Son!" Alysius urged, waving for him to follow.

Tice took one last look at Donald. "If ever I *can* come back 'n see ya', I will," he said.

Donald broke down and took three steps to his friend and hugged him. Tears streamed down both boys' faces.

"Boys," Reuben said. "Time's of the essence. Hurry now!"

Donald and Tice separated, looked at each other, then laughed.

"Crybaby," Donald sniffed, wiping at his nose with the back of his hand.

"Naw, you!" Tice said and stepped away toward Alysius and the waiting carriage, managing just one look back and a wave. "Thank you, rev-rund 'n you, too, sir."

"Hold on, Tice." Donald opened the saddlebags, pulled out Tice's satchel and handed it to Tice.

Reuben, Reverend Randall and Donald all waved goodbye.

Alysius directed Tice to jump in the back of the carriage, where he had opened a hidden compartment. Tice squeezed his length in and pulled his satchel tight to his chest. He waved weakly with one hand and Alysius closed and latched the compartment door.

Within seconds they were gone, Alysius cracking a whip over the head of his horse. Within a minute, Tice could feel the carriage turn right onto another street, and shortly afterward turn right again and head slightly downhill. In his head he figured they were traveling back down the slope toward the oceanfront.

For Tice, the ride was rough, exacerbated by the tight quarters and darkness. He was glad to hear Alysius call "Whoa!" to the horse and gladder still when Alysius opened the compartment and said, "C'mon, son. Hurry."

Seconds later, the older man hustled Tice into a majestic, three-story home where an elderly maid held open the back door.

Tice noticed the lady was wearing an outfit. It's like ones worn by the slave women on Massah and Misses' mansion, he thought, but she ain't black. She's white. A white slave? Hm-m-m.

Tice noticed they stood in a large kitchen, with pots and pans hanging from the ceiling, two large brick ovens built into one wall like Massah had back home, a large double sink and all kinds of oversized forks and spoons and funny items he had not seen before.

The little lady quickly assessed Tice and turned to Alysius. "Wait here, Alysius," she said with surprising authority and walked out of the room, closing the door behind her.

Tice was used to the routine—being rushed in and out of homes, usually in the dead of night but sometimes in daytime like today. Yet he had never saw a house as big as this one. Unless one of those in Boston was this large.

Alysius turned to Tice. "Son, this is the home of General Samuel Fessenden. He's a lawyer. He's in the state Legislature. And he's an abolitionist; that means he's against slavery. And he does everything he can t' help folks like you escape. So, do whatever they ask, okay?"

"Yes-sir."

"In a minute, when that fine lady returns, I'll be leavin'. I probably won't see you again. This is my message to you: Trust in God, son. Trust in God and He'll never let ya' down. People might let ya' down. Yep, they surely will. But He never will. Never ever."

Tice nodded. "I do love 'n trust the Lord, sir."

"Good."

Just then the kitchen door opened and in swept a woman who Tice guessed was the mistress of the house. She was tall and thin. Curly graying hair framed a sweet face that nearly sparkled at Tice. She turned to his companion. "And who do we have here, Alysius?"

"Name's Tice and he's a fine young man lookin' t' move north t' freedom, ma'am. Mister Ruby told me t' bring him here in a hurry."

The lady looked questioningly at Tice.

"My Massah's man Morgan is close behind, ma'am," Tice offered. "We saw him at the church in town promisin' the min-ster he'd catch me. If he does he'll wail on me with his hoss whip for sure, 'n I heard him say he'd skin me alive if he caught me."

Mrs. Fessenden flinched. "We'll have none of that, Tice." She introduced herself and nodded toward the maid, "and this is our maid, Harriet. She'll show you to a hiding place."

Mrs. Fessenden turned to Alysius. "We have another runaway with us and will be moving him out tomorrow. It appears Tice will be joining him on his journey."

"I'll let Mister Ruby know, ma'am. Thank you." Alysius patted Tice on the shoulder. "Remember what I said—and go with God, son."

"Thank you, sir. I will," Tice said.

•••••

Watching Alysius walk out the door was like closing another chapter in his book of flight for Tice. Misser and Misses Randauf's gone, he thought. Misser Conrad's gone. Misser James from 'sylvania 'n Misser and Misses Brickett from New York and the Hill family from Mass'chusetts, they's all gone, 'n the others right up to Donald is gone. What's next?

Pappy, you watchin' over me? he prayed silently. Are my angels protectin' me? They'd better be, with Morgan on my tail. He shivered at the thought of the man whose very existence meant meanness.

Harriet motioned to Tice to follow her. She hurried down a hallway, turning up some steep stairs.

"This is the back stairway to the maids' quarters," she said. "There's just two of us. Cook and me and cook's gone to care for her ailing mother for awhile. Hurry, child, hurry."

Tice was surprised. *This little old lady is climbing these stairs like she's goin' downhill.*

When they reached the top of the stairs she pointed to the right. "Our rooms are that way. Come this way. Several steps down the hall, she stopped and grabbed hold of a painting that hung on the wall, then opened it like you would a book cover. She pulled the painting outward and Tice noticed it was on a hinge. Opening the painting exposed a door knob.

Harriet knocked on the wall three times, then turned the knob and, to Tice's amazement, a portion of the wall opened like a door. He looked up and down the hallway to see if he should have been able to spot the door. The walls were papered and the vertical lines of the design on the wallpaper were such that it hid the existence of the door.

Harriet turned to Tice and waved him past her. Another steep stairway, this one narrower than the other, led up to the attic level.

"Freeborn?" Harriet called quietly. "Freeborn, it's Harriet."

"I'm right here, Miss Harriet." The voice was deep and rich. Tice guessed the man was older than him. When he reached the top of the stairs right in front of Harriet he discovered he was correct. A broad-shouldered black man rose from a cloth-covered chair at the far side of a room that was about 10 feet wide by twelve or fourteen feet long. A small window looked out on the world. As the man stood, Tice watched in astonishment. The man had to bend over so as not to bump his head on the roof. This fellow is big! Tice thought.

"Freeborn, this is Tice. Tice, Freeborn," Harriet said.

Freeborn took two very long steps toward Tice and extended his very long arm. His hand enveloped Tice's. Tice felt at once both in awe and apprehension about such strength and also thankful this man would be at his side as they traveled together.

Freeborn smiled at Tice, displaying large teeth with a big space between the two front ones. "Freeborn's my new name," he said. "Just changed it yesterday. Ain't never gonna be a slave ag'in."

"Amen to that," Tice said.

"I'll leave you two to get to know one another," Harriet said. "I'll bring dinner up when it's time."

"Thank you, ma-am," Tice said.

Chapter Six
New Chapter Unfolds

After dinner that night, Samuel Fessenden visited the two men. He was Tice's height, about five-foot-ten, athletic and possessed a dignified, handsome face. Silver streaks through his thick dark hair told Tice that he wore his seventy-something years of age very well. He sported a black vest over a white, high-collared shirt like he belonged in a courtroom, but was obviously comfortable sitting with two black men.

"Tomorrow, gentlemen. Before the sun rises, we move you out," he said. "Tice, I just spoke with Reuben Ruby and he tells me a slave hunter is in town keen on finding you. Reuben said the man—"

"Morgan," Tice cut in anxiously.

"Yes, Morgan and another man had been checking the docks all afternoon. Then late in the afternoon he stopped in on Reuben's hack stand." Samuel chuckled. "As if he'd get any information out of Reuben, of all people. Ha!"

Tice and Freeborn smiled along with Samuel.

"I trust Reuben like I trust my three sons," Samuel said. "And I feel like every one of you young men and women who escape this far north are like an extended family of my own."

"You've three sons, sir?" Tice asked.

"Samuel Junior, Thomas and William. A pastor and two lawyers. William was just elected a United States Senator. I'm proud of all of them. And they're all severely against slavery.

"The Abolitionist Movement's strong here in Portland," Samuel continued. "Mariners', First Parish, Quaker and Abyssinian church leaders; owners of hack stands, barber shops and clothing stores; prominent people and not-so-prominent people, working together secretly to move slaves northward to Canada. Some of them were freed slaves themselves who had settled, legally, here."

"Freed slaves?" Tice asked in wonder.

Samuel nodded in the affirmative. "Several of them." He rubbed his hands together. "So, men, get a good sleep tonight. I'll be up to wake you when we're ready to go."

"Where we goin', sir?" Freeborn asked.

"North. That's all I can tell you."

"Can'da?" Tice asked.

"Yes, Canada."

"Colder there?" Freeborn asked.

Samuel laughed. "Yes, colder there."

"Black people there?" Tice asked.

"Yes, black people there. Those who help you into Canada will make connections for you. But beware, you're not safe yet. Don't ever believe you're entirely safe until you pass over our borders.

"Borders?" Tice asked.

"Leave the United States and enter Canada. There are abolitionists here and there, everywhere. But the law is the law and the law now says slaves are the property of the slave owners."

"Property?" Tice asked.

"Your master owns you like he owns a watch, son."

"'N a watch never stops runnin'," Tice said, his mouth twisting into a grimace.

"Well, Tice, before long, if all goes well, you won't need to run any more." Samuel patted him on the shoulder and smiled. "Sleep well, my boy."

After Samuel left, Tice lay down with Freeborn on side-by-side cots and they shared their stories.

"While you were pickin' the cotton fields I was workin' the Mid-Lothian mines in Virginia," Freeborn said, "for a man named Burnette.

"Mines?" Tice asked.

"Coal mines. Black, nasty stuff deep in the ground."

Tice wrinkled his nose. "Sounds harder'n my cotton fields."

"Neither one's *my* dream," Freeborn said. "One day there was a great 'splosion in the pump shaft. Ka-boom!"

Tice's eyes opened wide.

"Well, it killed fifty-five of us. Nearly got me, too. I barely 'scaped. So that night, after they told us-uns who was alive all the names of those-uns who died, I decided I'd 'scape altogether so's my name wouldn't be read next time there was a 'splosion."

"Next day I walked right out of the mine, right past the foreman and right off the property. He must've thought I was goin' to the latrine but I didn't stop. No sir-ree. Matter of fact, when I got out of sight I ran. Ran faster'n I ever thought I could run. Ran so long that I thought these here legs weren't really legs t'll, but just stumps—stumps that would burn up. And they burned like they might. Ran so hard they should-a fallen off."

"I knows that feelin'," Tice said.

"Yeah. I ran for a coupla days, stoppin' only to drink from a brook or river or to eat berries off a bush, hidin' out in underbrush 'n places when I slept, movin' out by night, sleepin' by day. Then—hi-ho!" Freeborn sat up straight. "I tell ya' what, Tice, I ran smack-dab into the Army."

"Army?"

"Yes-sir, the United States Army. There was prob'ly a hundred of 'em, all on horseback. Well, not all of 'em, but most. Followin' along with the Army was a dozen or so runaway slaves—just like me!"

"Why's they there?" Tice asked.

"Well, they figured they'd follow the Army 'cause the Army was headin' away from the South. 'N the Army hired 'em on as cooks 'n grooms 'cause that's what they did back on their plantashuns."

"Why didn't the Army pack 'em off back to their plantashuns?"

"Listen on and I'll tell ya'."

"What chore'd you do for 'em?"

"I was a groom," Freeborn said proudly. "I loves horses 'n they loves me. I could live on a horse."

"Yeah?"

"Yeah."

"Well, what happened then?"

"I was happy as a lark, thinkin' I was safe with all them men with guns 'n swords—o-o-h, big swords. Some of 'em even said their fam'lies owned slaves, but they was good with me.

"There was a preacher man there, too. Fella named Twichell, who teached us slaves—us free men, that is—'bout God 'n things."

"Yeah?"

"Yeah."

"You said you was thinkin' you was safe—but you weren't?"

"Well, ya' see, the big genr'l—his name's Hooker—was against slavery so he welcomed us. But 'nother genr'l, Sickles was his name, was a Democrat and them folks are most 'n large *for* slavery. So we's on a tightrope, you see."

Tice didn't know tightrope from hemp rope, but he nodded in agreement.

"Well, one afternoon we 'n the cavalry was camped in this field 'n we heard this sharp 'pang' like from a pistol."

"Pistol?" Tice pushed himself up and leaned on his elbow.

"Gun." Freeborn's eyes widened as he recalled the moment. "All of a sudden there was this ruckus 'n one of my friends, Israel, comes a-runnin' up the path, out of breath, holdin' his hat in his hand and scared out of his skin. 'They's shootin' at me! They's shootin' at me!' he hollers as he passes the gate to the camp.

"Then one of the sol-jers says to us freemen, 'Run, boys! Hide in the woods!' So's we did. We run. We hid—'n we listened as this group of men—slave hunters 'n some slave owners, too—on horseback came ridin' up."

Freeborn took a deep breath. "Then this Corpr'l Gilbert, who was standin' at the gate, shouts at them riders, 'Take one more shot and it will be to commit suicide!' Well, them riders stopped right there, in that clearin' in front of the gate. I was a-peakin' through a bush 'n saw it all, Tice."

"Yeah?" How could a fella this big hide behind a bush? Tice wondered. "Musta been a big, big bush!" he said.

"Ha!" Freeborn laughed. "Yeah, it was. Well, the sol-jers in the camp came together on that spot. One of them riders handed a paper to Corpr'l Gilbert. The paper had given 'em the okay to search the camp and, if they found any of us freemen, they could take us without the Army stoppin' 'em."

"Yeah?"

"Yeah. Then the maj'r who's in charge walks up, looks at the paper, shakes his head 'n finally says, 'Nine of you's can come in.' He didn't wanna let 'em in, but he had to, he told us later."

"Who's the paper from?" Tice asked.

"Hooker, of all people."

"Yeah?"

"Yeah. I don't understand that, neither. Anyhow, into camp comes these rich white men on their horses, actin' high-'n-mighty as if'n they was on an errand from the *Al*mighty. As if'n they was doin' *jus*tice. As if'n they was good 'n honest men. As if'n not lookin' mean, they weren't. 'N then, Tice, 'n then—"

"Yeah?"

"'N then, when them slave owners 'n their hired hunters reached the middle of the camp, them sol-jers closed in 'round 'em. Them hunters didn't know what t' do. Surely the sol-jers wasn't goin' to help 'em. Even those'ns who'd said they was okay with slavery. All the sol-jers looked mad, their faces scrunjin' up—"

Tice laughed as Freeborn made a face to show how the soldiers looked, with brows knit and fire in their eyes. "Yeah?"

"Yeah. Pol'tics went kaput. South 'n North went kaput. They's all *for* us-uns—us freemen—rather than *for* slavery."

"Yeah?"

"Yeah. Then such cussin' as I never heard started to be shouted at these slave hunters. Oh, Lordy! Then, of a sudden, Genr'l Sickles happens to ride into camp, hears the noise 'n asks the preacher Twichell what's goin' on. Preacher tells him and Sickles asks to see Genr'l Hooker's letter. Twichell tells him 'bout my friend bein' shot at, and Sickles gets angry and hollers, 'Get 'em out of camp at once!'

"Well, of a sudden, when the sol-jers hear this they

start shoutin' and cheerin' and begin tossin' things at 'em—apples, sticks, even chunks of dirt."

Beaming, Tice stood up and cheered. "You serious?" he asked.

"Serious."

"Then what?"

"Well, them slave owners 'n hunters didn't wait 'round. Their horses began to rear up and skitter this way 'n that. The sol-jers got closer 'n closer and they didn't have no jokes on their faces, neither." Freeborn smiled at the memory. "Sol-jer close 'nough for me to hear throws an egg at 'em 'n calls out, 'There's a look at the nobility of the land, friend—confused and ungraceful-like. We're all good getting' rid of 'em.' Then he laughs 'n throws 'nother egg."

"Serious?"

"Serious. 'N when we all felt safe to walk back into camp we was welcomed with cheers 'n hand-shakin'. T'was somethin' to 'sperience, t'was."

"Wow!"

"Yeah. Wow!"

•••••

An hour later, the two runaways were asleep, Tice enjoying visions of Army soldiers lined up along both sides of a city street cheering him as he walked between them.

Before he knew it, there was a knock at the door at the bottom of the stairs and he heard the door—or was it the wall?—open.

"Gentlemen?" It was Samuel's voice. "Freeborn. Tice. It's time to pack up and go. Got to get you out of town before the sun rises and that's about an hour away.

Within minutes, Mrs. Fessenden and Harriet had

filled Tice's and Freeborn's backpacks with food and they had lifted their backpacks, along with their daypacks filled with clothing, onto the flat bed of a buckboard and had scrambled up themselves. A middle-aged white man was sitting on the seat with the reins for two horses in his hands.

Samuel spoke quietly to the man, then stepped back to Tice and Freeborn. "Godspeed, gentlemen. Jeff here will take you north. May the Lord have His angels watching over you."

"Thank you, sir," Tice said to the man on the wagon.

"I'll never forget you, Misser Fessenden," Freeborn said.

"Me, neither," Tice said.

The Fessendens and Harriet waved goodbye and in seconds the buckboard was out onto Congress Street. Within minutes they were in the country, riding alongside Casco Bay northward. Little was visible under slim light from a fingernail moon.

"Sure diff'rent than ridin' on the back of a horse," Tice said as they bumped up and down.

"Sure diff'rent than walkin'," Freeborn replied.

"Serious." This time it was a statement, not a question. Complaint wasn't in either man's mind. Tice felt thankfulness escaping from Morgan and his master and expectation as to what lay ahead.

"Fellas," said the man named Jeff on the buckboard seat, "soon enough you'll probably both get to experience both riding *and* walking. Do you see that star up there? The brightest one?"

Tice and Freeborn followed the direction of Jeff's finger.

"Yeah," they said in unison.

"That's the North Star. That's the beacon, your heavenly guide in case you get separated from those who know the way. Follow that star and you'll reach freedom."

"Okay, sir," Tice said.

"Good. Now, get what rest you can and I'll deliver you to your next safe house. 'N you can call me Jeff if you'd like."

"Pleased to meet ya', Jeff," said Tice who still was not used to speaking to a white person so casually.

·····

As they rode on, Freeborn looked intently at Tice and asked, "What's your story? How'd you escape, anyhow?"

"The plantashun's in K'tucky. I swimmed a river into Ohio—'n I never swum before—to get away from Massah. Nice white people helped me 'scape. Then others, then others."

Tice smiled at the thought of all the faces that flashed before him, then continued: "Just awhile ago I was in Mass'jusetts. Been sleepin' in folks' attics, next to chimneys, behind walls that weren't walls t'all, or behind bookcases of bottles 'n veg'ables. In the middle of the night someone'd walk me or ride me to 'nother place and toss rocks at a window to let people know we's there so's they'd let us in. Sometimes people would give me a shirt their sewin' bee'd sewed, though the only bees I ever seen made honey, not clothes."

Jeff, listening in, chuckled along with Freeborn.

"Good people—'n the good Lord—helped me all the way. 'N one of 'em is now my brother."

"Yeah?"

"Yeah. My brother in the Lord."

"My Momma taught me 'bout the Lord."

"My Pappy taught me."

"Then how do we get to be brothers?" Freeborn

asked.

"Simple as just bein', I think," Tice said. "We is what we is. If you're close to God and I's close to God, then I knows I can trust you like I'd trust my brother if'n I had un."

"Well, I does have un, somewhere I don't know where now."

"Well," Tice offered his hand, "now you got 'nother un, okay?"

Freeborn took his hand in his own huge mitt. "Okay!"

•••••

Hours later as they neared another safe house in Topsham neither Tice, Freeborn, nor Jeff knew what was happening in Portland.

Millie Fessenden was upstairs in her sewing room when the front-door knocker, shaped like a lion with a lamb snuggled beneath his great head, began banging. The noise quickly became forceful hammering.

She heard Harriet call from the first floor, "I'm coming. I'm coming!"

Millie walked to the top of the stairs and watched as Harriet opened the door. Millie peered into the foyer and caught a glimpse of Police Chief Charles Pigeon and a hulk of a man standing beside him.

"Harriet," Pigeon acknowledged the maid. Millie noticed Pigeon tip his hat to the maid but the man beside him did not.

"Mister Pigeon." Harriet was obvious in her disinterest in the man.

"Misses Fessenden home?"

"May I tell her your business, Mister Pigeon?"

"Hidden slaves, Harriet."

"Slaves?" Harriet sounded astonished.

"Yes, slaves, Harriet. Now may I see your mistress"

"I'll get her."

As she turned to go, Morgan began to step through the doorway. Harriet turned back on him. "You stay here," she said with such force for the little woman that it stopped a surprised Morgan mid-stride.

Harriet turned to walk up the stairs, but Millie was already halfway down.

"Mister Pigeon," she said. The pronouncement carried an air of aversion.

"Millie—" Pigeon began but caught himself quickly at the piercing look he received from her. "I mean, Misses Fessenden—"

"Yes?"

"Ma'am, Mister Morgan here is from Kentucky and is looking for a slave. He has demanded, as is within his rights, the help of the law under the Compromise Act in routing out this runaway."

"And you're at my door." It was a declaration, not a question.

Morgan interrupted. "My questioning has led me to your house. I'd like a look inside."

"A look inside?" Millie Fessenden did not flinch.

"Yep."

Millie ignored Morgan and looked directly at the police chief. "Do you have that militia behind you, Mister Pigeon? The one the mayor called in to shoot innocents in our streets?"

The Portland Rum Riot had happened five years ago, in 1855, and, despite her efforts to do so, Millie Fessenden still had not forgiven Pigeon.

Pigeon winced. "Millie—Misses Fessenden, you know I did not do that. That was Mayor Dow's idea."

"An idea you allowed, sir. You're the law and expected to protect Portland's citizens and yet you allowed the militia to tromp into our streets, lift their rifles and shoot into a crowd of people.

"But they were getting violent."

"And who raised that violence to a whole other level?"

Millie Fessenden's temper rose at the recollection of the hostility which came about because of anger over a state law outlawing the sale of alcohol. Portland's large number of Irish immigrants took the law, four years old in 1855, as a thinly veiled attack on them.

Anger had bubbled over into aggression when Dow authorized the city to buy $1,600 worth of medicinal and mechanical alcohol for pharmacists and doctors and ordered it stored in a city-owned building.

Millie and Samuel happened to be strolling in town, shopping for a new dress for an anniversary party and unknowingly stepped into a crowd of people outside the building holding the alcohol.

They found out later that the gathering had grown from about 200 to 3,000. And when they turned a corner into the assembly, shoving and rock-throwing had started. Unbeknownst to everyone, a fearful Mayor Dow had called out the militia. After ordering the protesters to disburse, the militia detachment fired into the crowd.

Samuel had pushed Millie to the ground and hunkered over her, protecting her. She was shaken to the bone, fear overwhelming her. She had never faced anything like that in her life.

When the gunfire ended, a sailor, John Robbins, was found shot dead. Several others were wounded and rushed to the hospital. The incident angered Samuel beyond anything Millie had ever seen and, within herself, fear had mutated to fury.

Dow? Pigeon? To her, they were as much at fault as the militia. A man had died! Samuel had been one of many outspoken critics of the police chief as well as the mayor, despite Dow being a longtime friend and slavery opponent. Now, Pigeon stood before her.

Millie was still awaiting an answer from a dumbfounded Pigeon when Morgan interrupted.

"Lady, I'm coming through," he snarled, bringing his right arm from behind his back. In his hand was a bullwhip.

Millie gasped.

"Morgan," an alarmed Pigeon said, "we'll have none of that. Put that whip away, or I'll put you away in jail for threatening behavior."

Morgan's eyebrows knit together. A storm obviously brewed behind them. Millie watched as he clenched and unclenched his left fist, then wrapped it around the cracker, fall and thong of the whip. He stared at Pigeon but the policeman did not wilt under that gaze like so many did.

"The Fessendens are honored citizens of this city, Morgan. I will allow no threats here," Pigeon said. He turned to Millie. "May we just have a quick look around, if Morgan here leaves his, ah, comfort blanket outside?"

At that, Harriet, who had stood back in the foyer, objected, "Misses Fessenden, no!"

Millie held up a hand to Harriet, then nodded to Pigeon. "First floor, yes. Other than that, no. The second and third floors are our private rooms."

Morgan grumbled loudly against the restriction, but Pigeon cut him off. "Agreed."

Millie stepped aside and held Harriet's hand in hers.

"But, chief," Morgan complained, "the little blackard could be just above us and we couldn't find him!"

"I assure you, mister slave hunter," Millie said, "there is no 'little blackard' here. Nor is there any person who is or has been a slave.'"

"You say," Morgan spat out.

"I notice you can see *some* plain facts," Millie responded.

"As plain as that if you are an 'honored citizen' of this city I'll be glad to be movin' on."

"Then be at it and be gone," she said. "When you do, take your bad behavior and impolite manners with you."

Morgan glowered at her and tromped past. He spent the next several minutes stomping from room to room. When he reappeared, he made for the door. Following Pigeon out the doorway, he turned to Millie. "I'll find the darkie, no thanks to you. And I'll make sure every honest slave hunter in Kentucky knows about this house of yours."

"Thank you for the advertisement," she said and shut the door in his face.

When Millie turned from the door Harriet walked up and hugged her. The embrace lingered as they prayed together for Tice's and Freeborn's safety.

•••••

Morgan walked back to the police station with Pigeon. Once inside he approached a map of Maine on the big wall behind Pigeon's desk.

"Where do they go?" he asked.

"Runaway slaves?"

"That's who I'm after, chief."

"You've traveled this far and you've not caught the boy yet, but you're still willing to travel into the wilderness of Maine after him?"

"Chief Pigeon, catching the little runaway has caused me no end of grief. I've been away from home for months now. Months! When I get my hands on him, I'm going to unleash a fury the little bag of dirt could never imagine. It's no longer a job. It's retribution."

Pigeon lowered his eyes. "I see."

"So where do they all go?"

Pigeon stepped to the map. "If they don't leave by boat it's guesswork at this point. Take the wrong route and you can forget it. This is Maine, not New York. North of here is woods, woods and more woods all the way to where they're headed, which is Canada, and any roadways ain't close together, for sure."

"What are the choices?"

Pigeon pointed to the northwest of Portland. "This direction on toward Montreal."

He pointed directly north. "This way on toward Quebec."

He pointed along the coast to the east. "This way to New Brunswick."

Morgan pointed first to the northwest. "Eeny meeny—" then to the north "miney moe—"

Pointing to the east along the coast, he said with finality, "That's where I'm going—to catch a little blackie by the toe."

With that, Morgan turned on his heel and walked out the door. He kept the bullwhip looped in his belt, and hoped that anyone, slave or free, who caught a glimpse of his beefy arms and broad shoulders would feel a shudder down their spine. He liked that feeling—as an instiller of fear. He growled to himself and a smile played quickly at the corner of his mouth.

•••••

Two days later, on their way from Topsham to Augusta in the middle of the night, Tice and Freeborn again looked up from the back of a wagon and spotted the North Star that Jeff had mentioned.

"There she is," Tice said, pointing to the brightest

light in the sky.

"Yeah? Where?"

Tice jabbed toward the sky with his index finger. "There. The North Star!"

"I sees it! Why you suppose they call it the North Star, anyway?

"Named for some man, I s'pose. The first man who spotted it. Maybe back when Jesus was born. Maybe it was the star the wise men followed to find the baby Jesus."

"So's maybe one of the wise men was named Mister North?"

Reuel Williams, sitting ahead of them and driving the two horses hitched to the wagon, laughed and looked over his shoulder. "Boys, north is a direction. Sailors, hunters, travelers of all sorts—like us, even— look for that star to know which direction is north instead of south, east or west."

"What's a direction?" Tice asked.

Reuel pointed directions. "That's north, just where the star is leading us.

"That's south, where we're coming from.

"That's east, to the Atlantic Ocean and the way your people came from when they were captured in Africa."

"That's west and into the wilderness."

"Is there a East Star?" Tice asked. "One I could follow back to where my Pappy's pappy came from?"

"'N my Daddy's daddy's daddy?" Freeborn added.

Reuel shook his head. "No, but if you face to the north, east will always be to your right, south behind you and west to your left. Okay?"

"Okay," Tice said.

"No matter," Freeborn said. "I don't wanna go no place where they catch people and make 'em slaves."

"Head north or east into Canada and you'll be safe from anyone catching you," Reuel said.

"Even Morgan?"

"Is that the man you mentioned who's chasing you?"

"Yeah."

"Well, even safe from him."

"How long before we get there?" Tice asked.

"You're still a ways away. A week if you could travel straight. But that won't happen. It's not easy getting there. Easiest would have been getting on board a ship in Portland, but the slave hunters are all over the docks—like ants on honey."

"We goin' to your home now?"

"Nope. Got a full house and it's a big house to fill up," Reuel said. "We've got fourteen rooms but have to be careful right now. Danger lurks. No, I'm taking you to the Nason homestead. Usually it's the other way around. Runaways go there first. We'll work it out. But," he hesitated, "it's best you don't know any of this."

"Causin' what we don't know we can't tell?" Tice asked.

"Correct."

"Causin' they could whip us and make us talk?"

"Correct."

Tice looked at the giant of a man beside him and smiled. "I don't think they'd be able to beat up my friend, Freeborn."

"You'd be surprised, Tice. It's not that we don't trust you young men, but these slave hunters have ways to get information that you truly don't want to know about."

Tice sat quietly, contemplating what sorts of things Reuel meant. Beside him, Freeborn was still, apparently lost in his own thoughts.

An hour later faint light was showing over the horizon, hinting at sunrise in a few short minutes as they rode along the east side of the Kennebec River and came to the outskirts of Augusta, a community set along its waters. Reuel told the runaways to cover themselves with the blankets and bags of potatoes. Then they rode into town. Another ten minutes on a nice country road and they came to the Nason homestead, a two-story average-sized home.

Frank Nason, a coat pulled tight about him, waved Reuel toward the back of the house where everyone quickly got out of the wagon and rushed into the house, Tice and Freeborn each carrying a daypack filled with clothing and backpack with the little that was left of their food supply.

Reuel and Frank shook hands, Reuel introducing the runaways. "Thanks for doing this wrong-way-around, Frank," he said. "I've got a full house. You're going to have to take these young men straight to Vassalboro if you can."

"Sure can."

"Let me know how it goes."

"Sure will, Reuel."

With that, Reuel hustled back to the wagon and was off back to Augusta.

"Follow me, young men," Frank Nason said. He shed his coat onto a wooden post on a wall, and they followed him through a ten-by-ten-foot shed, then a large kitchen and a dining room, past a steep flight of stairs and into a parlor.

Stoking fledgling flames in a fireplace was a woman who had obviously just awoken, wearing a bathrobe and with her hair askew.

"This is my wife, Mildred. I'm Frank."

Tice and Freeborn nodded. Mildred smiled in return.

"Sorry to hurry you through the house like this," Frank said. "The curtains are all pulled tight because we think there's an informer about and we're being extra careful."

"Informer?" Tice asked.

"We think someone has been sneaking around Augusta," Mildred Nason said, "perhaps more than one, perhaps many. We don't know, but we think someone has informed the police about a couple of safe houses."

"We have to keep you under wraps," Frank said.

Tice looked at him questioningly.

"Hidden from sight," Frank explained.

"Oh," Tice said. "We's used to that, ain't we, Freeborn?"

"Sure is," Freeborn shrugged. "I can't wait to be *over* wraps."

Frank and Mildred chuckled.

"Some day," Tice assured him.

"Some day soon, I hopes."

"Remember what Misser Reuel said. Maybe a week or two if we'uns hustle."

"Yeah. That's my dream."

"Well, my immediate dream," said Mildred, "is to get you safe and hidden, comfortable and fed—in that order."

"Over here," Frank said, directing them past a couch and several chairs to the back of the room. He pointed to a large bookcase filled with books of all sizes.

"Wow!" Tice said. "That's a lot of readin' to do. My brother Davey would love it here."

Frank tilted his head. "Your brother can read?"

"Well, not my real brother. He's a white boy, my brother in Christ. He was teachin' me t' read—that is, 'til I had to leave and run north to Portland. He'd love your-n's books."

"So, you can read."

"Some."

"Some enough to read this?" Frank took two steps to his right and pulled a book from a shelf near the floor. Handing it to Tice, he said, "Take a look and see if it's too difficult for you or not. If you can read it, it's yours."

"Wow!" Tice felt the book. Its cover was a fine leather that was soft to the touch. Looking at the title, he read self-assuredly, "*The Pilgrims Progress.*"

His eyes caught the older man's and Frank spoke, "It's about the long trek toward God and the spiritual freedom He offers. I think you're in the midst of your own long trek toward freedom.

"I knows. I got a copy of my own."

Tice read the startled look on Frank and Mildred's faces. "Nice lady in Ohio gave it t' me," he explained.

"Well," Frank said, "I'd say that along with the Bible it's a good book to learn to read by."

"I started readin' it to him," Tice pointed toward his friend, "didn't I, Freeborn?"

Freeborn nodded firmly. "Yeah, I like that."

"When you're reading it," Frank said, "think of this: the author of that book was in prison when he wrote it. He was in a dark, unfriendly place for preaching the gospel and yet he set out to share a story in that book that has saved men's souls. He was undeterred by his circumstances."

Tice didn't understand all the words but he felt he knew what Frank was conveying. "It's like not lettin' the runnin' and the scaredness and the thoughts of some old slave hunter keep you from havin' joy and 'speriencin' life, 'n friends 'n prayin' out to God."

"'N havin' a dream," Freeborn cut in.

"Yeah, 'specially that," Tice said.

Frank smiled broadly.

"Sit down and get warm before the fireplace," Mildred said, "and I'll bring you something to eat. You can eat it right here on the couch. But then you'll have to hide."

"Hide where?" Tice asked.

"Look here," Frank said. He walked to the corner of the bookcase, grabbed its edge at a certain place and pulled it toward him. As smoothly as the well-oiled workings of a clock, the bookcase moved on a hinge away from the wall. Frank stepped into the darkness behind it, struck a match and lit a hurricane lantern.

Tice and Freeborn stepped into a room probably six feet wide by the length of the parlor which was about twelve feet. A large mattress lay on the floor, from wall to wall at the left-hand side.

Tice turned to Freeborn, elbowed him in the ribs and laughed, "You're too tall."

"Naw, I sleep like a baby all curled up. Won't bother me none. But I do likes to see out of doors."

"I'm afraid that can't be done here," Frank said. "But we'll make you as comfortable as we can."

Tice and Freeborn followed Frank's direction into the room and set down their daypacks and backpacks.

"Follow me and while Mildred's getting your breakfast I'll show you the escape route," Frank said.

Stepping to the far right side of the hidden room, he knelt and lifted up a metal handle. A section of the floor rose up, revealing a ladder down into darkness. They followed Frank down the ladder and into the cellar. The floor was dirt, the walls large pieces of granite. They followed Frank to a short and narrow door at the back of the cellar.

"The house is on a hillside and this leads out," he said. "If you have to run for it and I'm not with you, hide in the woods, or head north or east. Okay?"

"Okay," Freeborn said.

"Follow the North Star," Tice added.

Frank nodded affirmation and patted Tice on the

shoulder.

•••••

Late in the afternoon, Tice was lying next to Freeborn on the mattress napping to catch up on the sleep they had lost the previous couple of days. The lantern, turned down low, shed scant light in the little room. Tice covered his head with his coat, trying to shut out Freeborn's snoring; it was so loud it reminded him of the train which he'd jumped on to escape Morgan back in Connecticut.

Suddenly there were three knocks on the wall. Tice sat up quickly, knowing that it was a signal from Frank or Mildred Nason. He jabbed Freeborn. "Stop your snorin', Freeborn, 'n wake up."

The bookcase moved, allowing faint light to filter in from the sitting room.

"Boys!" Mildred whispered loudly. Alarm filled her voice. "You must be quiet. Police are coming to the front door right now. Blow out your candle and don't breath a word until Frank or I come get you. If this bookcase begins to open before you hear three knocks, be on your feet to the cellar and out of doors with lightning at your heels."

Tice pulled himself to a standing position, fear alerting every sense. Freeborn moaned, wiped at his eyes and stood up.

"Better gets our shoes on, Freeborn."

"Sure 'nough."

•••••

Frank, just home from work, walked slowly through the foyer. At the front door, two police officers peered through the glass. A skinny lady wearing a flowered hat stood behind them.

Crazy Cate! *Cantankerous woman!* Frank thought when he spotted her. *Contention is your middle name!*

Frank glanced toward Mildred walking from the back of the parlor. She nodded approval to open the door, which he did.

"Officers," he said in greeting. He hesitated, unable to hide his disdain for the woman. "Cate."

"Sorry to bother you, Mister Nason," said one officer. "I'm Sergeant Whitestone. This here's Officer Shockey."

Nason nodded.

"We've heard a disturbing story," said Whitestone.

"What's that, officer?" Frank asked.

"That you're harboring slaves," he said matter-of-factly.

"And that's an offense of the law, a violation of the Fugitive Slave Law," Shockey said.

Mildred stepped beside Frank and took hold of his elbow.

"Uh-huh," Frank said. "And, Cate, is this your doing?"

Cate stepped through the door and replied, "Franklin, contempt for the law is contempt for all of us."

"Us who?"

"Why, us citizens of these American states." She stuck out her chin.

"And was it these individual states who agreed to this Runaway Slave Law?" Frank asked.

"Well—" she looked this way and that. It appeared to Frank that she was seeking the answer from some shadowy depths of her mind.

"It was the United States Congress," declared Shockey.

"Then our Maine legislators did not vote this act of

immorality?" Frank asked.

"No, sir, but whatever your feelings about it, it *is* the law of the land," said Whitestone.

"Do we not have states' rights, officers?" Frank looked each man in the eye.

Both lawmen shrugged, but apparently Cate had had enough time to consider the question. "It's a law for the 'greater good,'" she said.

"'Greater good'?" Mildred interrupted.

"Yes, Mildred. The 'greater good' of society. You can not deny that."

"And why can I not deny that?" Mildred asked, a trace of offense in her voice.

"If we in the North assist slaves running away from their rightful owners, we could incite war—a civil war, a war in which men die."

"So," Mildred said, "giving fleeing slaves over to the authorities may not be for the 'greater good' of those slaves but it will be for the *'greater good'* of their *'owners,'* plus it will avoid conflict."

"Correct." Cate nodded her head exaggeratedly.

"Cate," Frank cut in, "if you have a tumor do you have it removed?"

Cate flashed Frank an angry, odd questioning look. "Why, of course."

"Then if our country has a tumor should we remove it?"

Cate wavered. It was obvious she did not want to step into the hornet's nest where the question was leading.

"You call it a tumor. Others say slavery is vital to our nation's economy. And, last I looked, we're not an old country with riches stored through the ages. We're still a fledgling republic, Franklin."

"Ah-ha!" he said. "Republic!"

"Yes, republic."

"And what is a republic?"

Cate tossed up her hands.

"The 'people' speak," he said. "The 'people' decide. And, in this case our Articles of Confederation created a weak Federal government with very little, if any, authority to overrule state actions. Then the Tenth Amendment of the Bill of Rights gave states the right to oppose violations by the Federal government of Federal authority.

"No lesser men than Thomas Jefferson and James Madison wrote that the Federal Union is a *voluntary* association of states, and if the central government goes too far each state has the right to nullify that law."

Sergeant Whitestone held up a hand. "Excuse me, sir. But we do have to act on this accusation."

"Fact is," Shockey said, "the Supreme Court last year in the Dred Scott decision said one of the states' rights was protection of slave property wherever it went."

"I know," Frank said firmly. "A dastardly and cowardly decision. A decision that flies in the face of the Preamble of our Constitution that says 'all men are created equal.' A decision that essentially says these men and women who are held slaves have no rights—no rights at all."

"Well, then, I have no rights. Why should they?" Cate nearly screamed the question.

"Cate," Frank objected, "what are you—?"

"To vote. To hold a good-payin' job. To—"

"Cate!" Frank was flabbergasted. "Are you comparing your life to slavery?"

"For me, the shoe fits."

"Maybe that's the case, maybe not. But if it does, do you wish the same fate on others? Others who have no choice? Others who were captured, hauled in the hulls of ships to these shores thousands of miles from their homes, then made to work other men's fields for other men's profits, while they were treated like so much chattel?"

"Chattel is what they are. So says the law," she argued.

"You have no answer to my question so you raise another point," Frank declared. "Your arguments are moving targets, Cate. Gun one down and another pops up in another field."

"Nevertheless," Whitestone cut in, stepping between Frank and Cate, apparently in hopes to end the argument, "that is the law, sir—set down by the High Court. And the law is what Officer Shockey and I are sworn to uphold. That said, sir, may we come in to have a look around?"

With resignation, Frank and Mildred stepped aside.

"Please be hasty. We're expecting company," Mildred said.

"Ma'am—sir." Whitestone tipped his cap and walked past Frank and Mildred through the foyer into the parlor on the left.

"Ma'am, sir," echoed Shockey, tipping his cap and stepping past them to the right into the dining room.

Frank followed Whitestone into the parlor and feigned unconcern. He could overhear Mildred in the foyer speaking to Cate.

"Cate," Mildred said, "are you a churchgoer?"

"I'm not discussing this on those terms" was the angry response.

"Do you believe in God?"

"Yes."

"Then what would you say He would think of this?"

"He allowed slavery in the Bible."

"Yes. But if you look at the 'slaves' in the Bible they're given high positions, Cate. Joshua, a slave, even ruled Egypt for Pharaoh. The concept was so far removed from what we're allowing in America."

"Still, he was a slave."

"Yes, but he had rights, upward mobility. Daniel and his friends each ruled a large portion of Nebuchadnezzar's kingdom."

"So they got rights," Cate stated.

"Yes."

"Like I said afore, I don't even got no rights."

The conversation ended and a moment later Mildred entered the parlor, looked at Frank and shrugged. He cracked a crooked "can't-win-them-all" smile at her, then turned his attention to Whitestone, who was looking intently at the bookcase.

•••••

Inside their hiding place, Tice stood side by side with Freeborn, their ears to the back of the bookcase, trying to hear the goings-on in the room. Tice could faintly hear the voices at the front door, then the footsteps on the wood floor of someone entering the room and walking toward them, then a second set of footsteps.

Tice grabbed Freeborn by his massive biceps, his hands barely getting around the front of his arms but his fingernails digging in.

Freeborn winced, perhaps too loudly. Suddenly the footsteps stopped. Was someone dangerous on the other side?

"That's an interesting bookcase you have there," Tice heard a muffled voice say. "Floor to ceiling and nearly the width of the wall."

Frank's reply sounded like "Built it myself."

"You run a mill and you built it yourself?"

"Sure did. I like to work with wood."

"The titles of your books are impressive. Nathaniel

Hawthorne's *The Scarlet Letter*; William Penn's *No Cross, No Crown*; a book of stories by Hans Christian Anderson."

A muted reply.

Tice could hear what sounded like a hand sliding along the bookshelf at chest height.

"Do you see … borrow?" It was Frank's barely audible voice again. "I've … them all… no haste…returning."

Tice again heard footsteps on the wooden floor. The person was stepping closer.

Will he notice the hinges? Tice wondered.

•••••

Frank tried to remain calm as Whitestone ran his fingers along the bookcase. He leaned forward and looked intently behind the books, then ran his hand along the edge of the bookcase. Frank held his breath. With startling quickness, Whitestone turned on his heals and looked directly in Frank's eyes. "I guess I'm through in here," he said, hesitating and seemingly trying to read Frank's reaction. "I'll catch up with Charlie."

After Whitestone strode past him, Frank blew a sigh of relief then followed him through the foyer.

"Nothing in there," Whitestone said to Cate and headed toward the dining room.

Cate's brow knit into a scowl.

Walking by Cate, Frank looked intently at her. "I don't understand you, woman," he said. "What motivates you?"

"The law!" she said. "What motivates you? Lawlessness?"

"No. Integrity," he answered and followed Whitestone to the parlor. Mildred stepped quickly to catch up to the two men.

•••••

Cate watched them, and almost took a step in their direction. Then her left eye twitched and she turned her eyes to the parlor. An odd feeling came over her and she slid into the parlor. She stood, taking in the room in its entirety—a fireplace on the outside wall, faced by a brocade sofa, with a winged-back chair at either side; two floor-to-ceiling windows; a writing desk between the window on the right and a large bookcase. A very large bookcase. Very large. Hm-m.

She squared her hat on her head and walked with purpose to the near floor-to-ceiling wood structure. Something drew her to walk directly to the far-right side of the bookcase. Once there, she gave it a tug. "Oh!" she gasped as the bookcase, which must have weighed hundreds of pounds, swung smoothly toward her. *It's like a huge door!* she thought and stepped back, putting her right hand to her heart.

"What have we here?" she whispered. It was too dark to see inside very well, but it was definitely a secret room of some sort.

She stepped inside and looked around, waiting for her eyes to adjust to the dark. Slowly she could make out a mattress on the floor. Then a small round table. Something on the table. She bent down to pick it up. A book. Nothing else.

Cate stepped back out into the parlor, her eye twitching. She studied the book in her hand. *The Pilgrim's Progress.*

•••••

Meanwhile, Frank didn't want Whitestone out of his

sight. Whitestone found Shockey in the kitchen and told him to check the upstairs rooms.

Shockey complained and tromped up the flight of stairs.

Whitestone put his hands on his hips and looked around the room. A shudder of fear flew down Hank's back. Had Mildred left something in the kitchen that would point to Tice and Freeborn? His eyes soared around the room, then slowly scanned it. No, nothing! Phew!

"What's back here?" Whitestone said, pointing behind the kitchen.

"Oh, the shed."

Whitestone stepped into the entry room. Boots sat on the floor by the door, coats hung on wooden pegs, a spade and a snow shovel leaned against a wall.

Suddenly, it appeared that Whitestone noticed a movement through the lone rear window. He stepped quickly to the window, pulling aside curtains to look out.

Frank looked over his shoulder. Through the window.

Two black men running to the woods!

Eyes wide, Whitestone twirled around to look at Frank.

"Sir!" he breathed.

As suddenly as he had spun around, Whitestone turned back and looked again as the two men disappeared into the woods. He froze for a moment, then heaved a sigh.

What is he thinking? Frank wondered. *What is he doing?*

Then, as slowly as he had been quick, Whitestone reached for the curtain and pulled it tight. Turning back, he spoke, as if his mouth was filled with mud. "Mister Nason, I think we've taken up enough of you good folks' time."

Relief fell upon Frank as heavily as had the alarm that had made his heart race.

Just then, Cate shouted from the parlor.

When Frank, Whitestone and Mildred arrived at the parlor entrance, with Shockley running up behind them, they found Cate, one hand holding her hat on and the other pointing to the hiding space.

"There!" she hollered. "Look! There!"

Whitestone and Shockey strode to the dark space where she pointed.

"What have we here?" Whitestone asked, peering inside.

"Exactly!" Shockey said. "What is this place?"

Both men turned to face Frank and Mildred.

"Our children used to use it as a playroom, kind of a kids' hideaway," Frank said.

"Yes," Mildred added, "it was a, ah, wonderful place to stay concealed when they and the neighborhood children played hide-and-seek."

Shockey looked doubtful. Whitestone's lips curled slightly.

"Well, I'll be!" Cate exclaimed.

"And no one's been here since your children?" Shockey asked.

"To tell you the truth, officer, I completely forgot about it," Frank said.

"Pshaw!" A declaration more than an exclamation escaped Cate's lips. "What's this here, then?"

Cate pulled the copy of *The Pilgrim's Progress* from behind her back.

Frank hesitated, then spoke up. "Why, that's my book! Imagine that. That's where it disappeared to. I haven't seen it in years."

"Nah! T'isn't either!" Cate shot back. "You yerself taught my granddaughter from that book in Sunday

School just last year. I was told about it."

"Perhaps you might read it yourself, Cate," Mildred interjected. "The message might help you."

"Pshaw again! I don't need no help that way." Cate looked at Shockey. "You believe this tripe?"

Shockey shrugged.

"You?" she said, nodding at Whitestone.

"Makes sense to me," he said without emotion.

"Snakes and stones, sense and nonsense!" Cate declared as if she were addressing Congress. "Law be good and law be damned, but somethin's squirrelly here and it ain't no varmints that's doin' it, neither."

With that, she handed the book to Frank. "Pass it back to your friend who left it behind—if'n you can catch up to him, wherever he is."

"I don't know what you—" Frank began. But Cate dismissed him with a wave of her hand and stomped past him and Mildred and the two officers, out the parlor, through the foyer and out the front door, not even closing the door behind her.

"Humph," said Shockey. "Waste of time. We goin', Sarge?"

Whitestone nodded assent and winked at Frank as he passed by.

When the officers left the house, the door closing behind them, Mildred ran to Frank's arms. "Dear God, dear God," she whispered huskily. "Where'd they go?"

"Where do you think, hon? Back to the woods."

"Then you'd better go retrieve them."

"Give it a minute. Let the officers of the law leave. Let Hurricane Cate get home. Let darkness set in. Then I'll 'retrieve' them, if they haven't run far away."

Mildred grabbed Frank's elbow. "It scares me."

"What?"

"Well, how did Cate find out?"

"Don't know."

"And who else might know?"

"Don't know."

"That's what frightens me. We simply don't know. But somewhere there's a leak in the bucket."

"Well, I did discover today that we have a friend—or at least the probability of one—in an important place."

"Yes?"

Frank told Mildred about Whitestone spotting the slaves but not mentioning it. Mildred put her hand to her mouth. "Praise the Lord!"

•••••

When dusk fell, Frank already had two horses hitched to a wagon and Mildred had filled a burlap bag with foodstuffs—slices of meat pie wrapped in newspaper as well as a loaf of bread and hot coffee in sealed tankards.

Frank tied the reins to the buckboard seat, patted the copy of *The Pilgrim's Progress* just to remind himself to give it to Tice, then sauntered down the hill toward the woods. He was anxious and worried inside but wanted to appear casual on the outside in case someone saw him and wondered why he was wandering around a pasture at this time of night. Frank hayed this field to feed his horses, and the hay was only calf-high right now, so it was easy walking but he could barely see the outline of the trees ahead.

As he neared the forest he scanned the surrounds of the house behind him to see if anyone was about. No one in sight. Turning his attention back to the woods, he called out in a low tone, "Tice. Freeborn."

No movement, none at all.

"Tice. Freeborn."

Had they gone on? If so, where? Following the

North Star?

"Boys, it's me, Frank Nason."

Still nothing. Frank decided to walk to his left along the tree line. A few yards along, he stopped, stared into the ever-darkening forest and called again. "Boys, we've gotta go. We've got a long ride ahead of us and we have to go tonight."

Suddenly there was a rustling in the woods.

"Misser Frank?" It was Tice's light voice.

"Yes."

"We's right here."

"We's comin." It was Freeborn's deep-toned declaration.

"Good. Let's hurry."

Minutes later, their daypacks and Mildred's food loaded on board, the three men were on their way.

• • • • •

It was a good thing Frank Nason knew the way, Tice thought as they rumbled along a rough road southward, then turned eastward, entering deep forest.

Once they were a ways into the woods Frank spoke over his shoulder. "It's okay to get up now, fellas. You can come sit on either side of me here on the seat."

Tice and Freeborn gladly agreed, scurrying to sit beside their newest friend.

"Sure was scared back there," Freeborn said, a tight chuckle escaping his lips. "Like knowin' that the mine might fall down on ya' any minute."

"Mine?"

Freeborn told Frank about his long hard days working in the mines.

"That's awful!" Frank said.

"Made me strong, though," Freeborn said and flexed a huge biceps. It almost glistened under light from a moon that just emerged from behind a sky full of dark clouds.

"Sure did," Frank agreed. "When things change here in America, you can come and work for me anytime."

Freeborn laughed. "I've got offers, Tice. Thank you, Misser Nason. Thank you so much."

Frank turned to Tice. "And you, too, young man. I know you'd be a wonderful employee."

"Imploy-ye?" Tice repeated.

"Worker, son. A worker who gets paid money for his labors."

"Uh-huh." Tice nodded. "Thank you, sir."

"As I was walking down the pasture to find you young men I was wondering if you had taken off following the North Star," Frank said. "Of course when there's heavy cloud cover like it was earlier it's impossible to follow the North Star. But continue to read this book of yours," he placed *The Pilgrim's Progress* in Tice's hand, "and you'll get an idea how to find your way.

"The Lord's watching your every step. He's watching over us right now. Seek Him, speak to Him and listen quietly before Him and He'll guide you even better than that North Star."

"You suppose He was watchin' over us today when thems men came searchin' for us?" Tice asked.

"Yes-sir, He was."

"Then He watched good. Freeborn and I was leanin' up to the wall listenin' 'n I squeezed his arm real tight—"

"Dug it!" Freeborn cut in.

"Dug it," Tice agreed. "Well, Freeborn winced out loud and I swore people must've heard."

"Then we wondered what to do," Freeborn said, "to stay and be quiet or get down that there ladder and run."

"'N we grabbed our things and lit out like there was fire under our feet," Tice laughed.

"Hot coals ticklin' our toes!" Freeborn said.

"The tip of Morgan's whip whistlin' by my nose," Tice laughed, then caught himself short with the sobering thought, the possible reality of meeting up again with his adversary.

The ride got suddenly quiet until, a couple of hours later, they arrived at a white farmhouse. Good thing it was white, Tice thought, or they'd never been able to see it. The moon had appeared through the cloud cover only occasionally during the trip up and down hills that seemed to rise or fall forever. Even Frank's two huge workhorses strained to pull the wagon and three men up some of those inclines.

•••••

"Well, men," Frank announced at last, "we're here."

He pulled the horses to a halt. In the ever-so-dim starlight, Tice could see it was a beautiful manor fronted by five columns. "Wow!" he said. "What a man-shun."

"Ironically, it was built by a slave trader who died on a voyage to Africa," Frank said.

Good thing, Tice thought but didn't dare say.

"Stay here." Frank slipped past him and jumped down off the wagon.

Picking up a handful of small stones from the drive, Frank walked up beside the house and began tossing the stones lightly against a second-floor window. Pang. Ping. Pang.

Suddenly the window flew open and someone stuck their head out. "Who's it?" called a man's voice, short and crisp.

"Israel, it's Frank Nason."

"Frank?"

"Yes."

"I'll be right down."

Once everyone had piled into the house, Israel Weeks turned to Frank. "An informant tells me the sheriff is coming over here to search the premises today. You'd better head back soon. I'll get these young men over to the next station."

Frank nodded. "Law's been around our house, too. Who's stirring up this hornets' nest? Crazy Cate was with the police at my house, but it's got to be someone else—someone with power."

"Yeah, it does. I'll try to find out."

Minutes later, they were all headed off in different directions, a tired Frank Nason back to Augusta and Israel Weeks, Tice and Freeborn on board a wagon headed eastward toward a village called China.

Chapter Seven
A True Family Affair

After Israel Weeks delivered Tice and another slave, Freeborn, to Abel and Elizabeth Chadwick's, their big old rambling house became the slaves' home for three days. It was a whirlwind filled with both fun and games with the Chadwicks' three sons. Even the anxiety that had so often tightened Tice's stomach in knots seemed to take a vacation, the fear of the appearance of Morgan—his plantation's foreman, now slave hunter—largely evaporating in the giggles and games of fifteen-year-old Caleb, twelve-year-old Judah and nine-year-old Ephraim.

The first day they relaxed and played in a secluded back yard surrounded by thick bushes near the lawn and tall fir trees further away. It seemed an oasis.

Judah, overflowing with fun and daring, challenged Tice to stand on one end of a teeter-board and have someone else jump down on the other end from a height that must have been six feet!

Tice looked askance at Judah.

"C'mon, I've done it," Judah said, "'n I'm just a kid."

"That's why you done it, prob'ly," Tice laughed.

"No, really," Judah said. "It's fun. Do a flip while

you're in the air."

"A flip?"

"Yeah, go head over heels and land in that haystack there. It's a thrill!"

Tice's doubt took a twist in the direction of fear. "No-no-no, I'll let you be the massah of flips. Not me. I'll be the massah of watchin'."

All the boys laughed.

Caleb looked at Freeborn. "I usually jump down on the teeter-totter from that big rock beside it, he said, pointing to a boulder about six feet high. But you, Freeborn, if you jumped on it, boy what a ride *that'd* be for Judah."

Freeborn shook his head but the boys insisted. Over the next minute, the higher their rate of insistence the lower went his rate of refusal until, finally, he relented.

Freeborn climbed the rock, took aim on the narrow teeter-board and locked eyes with Judah. The boy had taken his post and was standing with a bend in his knees. He nodded okay and Freeborn, concentrating on his descent, jumped straight down on the board. He landed perfectly, sending the board down into the ground with a thud. Judah flew squealing into the air and landed on the haystack.

No longer had he landed then he jumped to his feet. "Again, Freeborn! Again!"

As Freeborn and Judah improved their talent at this new game, the others watched on, giggling and slapping hands. Caleb and Tice were too heavy to take Judah's place and Ephraim too little, but all three thrilled at the opportunity to cheer them on.

•••••

The second day, Abel Chadwick came home from work in the late afternoon to a laughing, cheering group of boys.

"Daddy, Daddy!" Ephraim said. "Guess what?"

Abel smiled. "What, son?"

"Freeborn's a tree!"

"A tree, is he?" Abel chuckled. He looked around at the other boys, then up at Freeborn. He had never seen a tree pitch-black like that, but then again he had never seen a man as big as Freeborn, either.

"Yep. And I'm a monkey," Ephraim added.

"That so?" Abel nodded. "I see."

"Yes," Caleb joined in, "and the rest of us are cheetahs 'n jaguars 'n mountain lions, just ready to grab him 'n eat him if he falls outta the tree."

"Ah-huh." Abel laughed. "Then why don't you eat him now since he's standing on the forest floor right in front of you?"

"Oh, Dad," Judah said with exasperation, "we just stopped the game long enough to catch you up on all the pert-nent informashun. Soon's you unnerstand, the monkey'll hop back up in the tree and we'll try to reach up 'n grab him again."

"Yeah, watch." Ephraim jumped up to grab Freeborn's arm which Freeborn had extended out to his side at waist height. Ephraim scrambled up, pushing his feet along Freeborn's leg, then pulling himself up and over.

Freeborn extended his arm until it was straight out and there sat Ephraim, one hand on Freeborn's shoulder and another on his elbow. "Ta-dah!" he said. "Now watch."

With that, he crawled across Freeborn's broad shoulders to the other arm. "Up, tree!" he ordered.

Freeborn raised his other arm straight up. Ephraim grabbed on, hand over hand, until he was squatting on Freeborn's shoulder and then standing, his tiny little hand engulfed in Freeborn's massive mitt. With victory gleaming in his eyes, he looked proudly at his father. Abel clapped his hands in applause.

"I'm king of the woods!" Ephraim asserted. "Monkey king!"

Caleb growled like a lion. "We'll see 'bout that!" And he reached up to grab a foot. But Freeborn stood up on his toes, putting Ephraim a hair out of his reach.

"I'll get him," declared Judah and he jumped. But he too fell short.

"Hm-m-m," Caleb said, "maybe we should tickle the tree."

"Tickle?" There was obvious hesitation in Freeborn's voice.

"Yes-s. Tickle."

Caleb nodded to Judah, who needed no more encouragement and each one started tickling Freeborn behind a knee. Giggling, then laughing, Freeborn started to topple. Finally he had to pull Ephraim down to his chest to avoid falling over. Then Caleb and Judah jumped to grab their little brother and all four fell laughing to the ground.

Abel chuckled at the heap of boys. Suddenly, he scanned the room and a frown covered his forehead. "Where's Tice?"

Caleb, recovering from devouring his brother just long enough to answer, said, "Oh, he's out helpin' Mom with the dinner, slicin' taters or somethin'."

"Tice is good with knives 'n things like that," Freeborn said. "I think I'd cut my fingers off."

"Well, that would take some knife!" Abel joked.

The boys all laughed. "Yeah, more like an ax," Judah declared.

Freeborn cringed. "I once saw a slave in the mine beaten with an ax handle. He was lucky there was no blade attached. He nearly died anyhow."

Abel decided to redirect the conversation. "Well,

boys, back to the monkey in the tree. I'll go check in with your Mom."

In the kitchen Abel found Elizabeth checking on a large chicken in the oven of a wood-burning stove. Tice was slicing carrots on a countertop.

As she tugged on a chicken leg with a gloved hand, Elizabeth spoke to Tice. "Yes, this town of China used to be called Jones' Plantation, named for a black man, a surveyor named John Jones, or 'Black Jones.'"

Tice stopped slicing and turned his attention to Elizabeth, then noticed Abel. "Oh, hello, Misser Chadwick."

Elizabeth shut the stove door. "I didn't hear you come in, dear."

Abel stepped toward his wife and they hugged.

"So you were telling Tice about John Jones." He looked at Tice. "Now there was a man you could relate to, young man. He was a man of daring and persistence."

Tice looked questioningly.

"Yes," Elizabeth said. "Almost a hundred years ago, back in the seventeen-seventies, when only Indians lived in these parts, Black Jones surveyed the territory."

"Surveyed?" Tice asked.

"He looked over all the land and mapped it out," Abel said. "Laid it out into a township."

"Then," Elizabeth said, "he persuaded people from southern Massachusetts to move here."

"The Clarks and Hatches," Abel said.

"The Fishes and Burrells," Elizabeth said.

"The Wards and Hamlins," Abel said.

"'N the Chadwicks?" Tice asked.

"Yes, and the Chadwicks," Abel said. "Most of us were related by marriage. Matter of fact, Israel Weeks who brought you here, is a relative."

"My family, the Starretts, came later," Elizabeth

said. "And my sister Susan married Abel's brother Joseph."

"Gee, a whole family and a family of families," Tice said. A wide smile dissolved slowly.

"What's the matter, son?" Abel asked.

"Oh, I was jus' thinin'. I got friends, but no fam'ly," Tice said. "Besides my Pappy, I got no kin. Aunt Isabelle ain't really my aunt."

Suddenly loud giggles and then cheers erupting in the other room interrupted them.

•••••

The third morning Tice woke up with the sun. Every new day the thought recurred to him: *They's no Morgan hollerin' to git up and git goin'. No hoein' to do. No cotton to pick. Nobody t'all givin' me orders. No achin' back. No achin' neck.* He looked at his calloused hands and thought of all the days they'd be bleeding when he dozed off to sleep.

This was freedom. He'd have to talk to Freeborn about this. *What must it be like to be free when you're born? To live all your life without nobody whistlin' a whip by your ear, or calling' ya godawful names, or makin' ya work until ya can't work no more 'cause there's no light to see by?*

What must it be like to go where you wanna go, when you wanna go as long as you wanna go and not be answerin' to no Massah? He thought of the chains that Morgan put around his Pappy's ankles every day and night for months after Morgan'd thought his Pappy was runnin' away. Of course Pappy wasn't runnin' away 'cause he wouldn't leave Tice behind. Never mind.

What must it be like to be workin' in the field and being able to get a drink of water whenever you wanted? To eat meals whenever you wanted? To go to bed and get up out of bed whenever you wanted?

What must that all be like? He was getting a taste of that freedom each and every day he left the plantashun further behind. Maybe that was what was going through Freeborn's mind the day he changed his name. Born free. Free born.

•••••

That evening they were all eating dinner together. Abel had heard rumors about a network of people who were as dedicated to helping slave catchers as were the people who were helping the slaves escape. And today co-workers at the gristmill were talking about slave hunters in the area. There would be no more playing outdoors for Tice and Freeborn.

Abel decided the runaways needed to be hidden until they moved out, and that had better be very soon. When he arrived home from work, afraid the slaves could be seen through the first-floor windows, he sent them to the second floor, where he pulled the curtains closed. The boys persuaded their parents to join Tice and Freeborn on the second floor so they could all eat together.

Between chews of chicken, Tice said, "We's so thankful for you folks."

"Sure is," Freeborn chimed in.

"Well, we're blessed to help out," said Abel, a muscular man who, Tice imagined, could lift even Freeborn off the ground a half foot. "The boys sure are glad, aren't you, sons?"

Nods around the makeshift table answered the question.

"We're thankful to the Lord for allowing us to help," said Elizabeth. "We know you want to get on your way, but there's trouble at the next stop."

"Trouble?" Tice asked.

"Yes. A runaway was caught with the family where we were going to take you. The people in that town are in an uproar—that someone from the South could come this far north and still be allowed to capture a, well, in this case a woman, and force her back to a plantation."

"Did they whip her bad?" Worry filled Tice's face.

"Don't know."

"They didn't skin her alive?"

Elizabeth flinched. "Tice!" It was spoken like the mother Tice never knew.

"Sorry, ma'am." Tice tucked his head down to his shoulder blades. "I—I heard Morgan said that's what he'd do to me if'n he catches me."

Abel, sitting to Tice's left, slid his chair next to Tice and put his arm around his shoulders. "Tice, son, we won't let that happen. Besides, Morgan's not going to catch you."

"Yeah, Dad," said Caleb, who was the image of his father, facially and physically, "you've got a horsewhip of your own."

"Bullwhip," Judah corrected.

"A *big* bullwhip," Ephraim added, stretching his arms wide to exhibit just how big it truly was.

Everyone laughed.

"Morgan'd sure feel the weight of *that!*" Tice exclaimed.

"Yep," Caleb said, "sure would."

"Yep," Judah agreed.

"Ah-huh," Ephraim said, crossing his arms as an exclamation point. "Sure would!"

Freeborn took a big bite out of a thick piece of bread, then set it down on his plate and looked around the table at the Chadwicks. A look of gravity filled his face. "Why y'all 'blessed' to help us. Why open your doors to us 'n treat us 'most like family?"

"Yeah," Tice said, "white folks and black uns don't mingle together where I come from."

"Tice, Freeborn," Abel said, "that's not the Lord's way."

"No?"

"No. Where did we all come from?"

"From our mommas."

"Yes, from our mommas. And the first momma was Eve. We all came from the same stock, Tice—from Adam and Eve. So we all *ought* to mingle. We shouldn't be separated by slave and slave-owner. Matter of fact, there should be no 'owners.' Even the Constitution of the United States of America says, 'All men are created equal.'"

"The Consti—?"

"The law of the land. The framework for our government."

"Uh-huh."

Abel looked sincerely at Tice. "Tice, you and Freeborn are just like the rest of us. So what if you have dark skin? Freeborn has even darker skin. I've got light skin and my dear bride," he smiled at Elizabeth, "has even lighter skin. Caleb over there," he pointed to his son across the table, "has darker skin than either Elizabeth or me. It's shades, son, shades from pure white to pure black—that's all. No matter our particular shade, God looks on us all as His beautiful creations. I'm sure He loves the black skin as much as the white."

"What about the red skin, Daddy?" Ephraim asked. "The Injun?"

"Red, too," Abel chuckled.

"Whenever you talk 'bout God," Tice said, "you look like trouble don't exist. You must know Him good."

Abel laughed. "Yes, son. You might have noticed

that we Chadwicks have every name in the Bible covered—kind of a sign post that we know our Maker well. Right here in this room we have Caleb, Judah and Ephraim—all famous Old Testament people. All around our family there is an Abraham, a Lot, a Paul—"

"And an Abigail, a Hanna, a Ruth—," said Elizabeth

"And a Daniel and a Job," said Caleb.

"And a Jotham and a James," said Judah.

"And a John and a Stephen," said Ephraim.

"Yes," Abel laughed, "and a Sarah, Lydia, Rebecca, Mary, Priscilla, Aaron, Naomi and Benjamin, to boot."

"Every once in awhile," Elizabeth said, "someone named their child Gear or Chloe or Charlotte or Rosannah."

"But we promptly kicked them out of the family," Abel declared.

"You what?" Freeborn gasped, and the Chadwicks all hooted.

"Nah, I was just kidding." Abel smiled broadly. "But we all do love the Lord and we all believe slavery is an evil that will curse our country if we don't declare it against the law."

"But, instead, the Northern states keep kowtowing to the Southern states and demanding runaways to be returned," Elizabeth said. "Nevertheless, many or most of us in the North look the other way when slaves come through. We don't tell the law and, a lot of the time, the law doesn't ask.

"'N sometimes people like you help us 'scape, too," Tice declared.

Elizabeth, sitting to Tice's right, patted him on the knee. "That we do, Tice. That we do."

"But I'm afraid that as much fun as we're all having with you in our house, danger's near our doorstep,"

Abel said. "So close that we need to be getting you packed and on your way."

"Oh, no!" The words escaped Tice's lips before he could stop them. He didn't want to endanger these nice people but he didn't want to go. He felt a tear quickly drop from his eye and start running down his cheek. This felt like home. This felt like family. This felt like a place he didn't never ever want to leave. He loved Elizabeth and Abel and Caleb and Judah and Ephraim. He loved them like he loved Donald.

Elizabeth put her arm around Tice's shoulders and drew him to her in a motherly embrace.

"I'm sorry. I'm sorry," he said as more tears joined the first one. "I don't wanna be no crybaby." But he could not control the emotions.

"It's okay," Elizabeth said. "I think we'd all like to cry."

"Matter of fact, we is." It was Freeborn, who was wiping away a tear and pointing to the boys who were all struggling with the news of their new friends' imminent departure.

"We didn't even get to play cowboys 'n Indians," Ephraim moaned.

"'N I wanted to show Freeborn my wooden train," lamented Judah.

"And Tice and I were reading *The Pilgrim's Progress* together. He's doing real well," Caleb added with what seemed to encapsulate everyone's feelings.

Abel stood to be heard. "Listen, children, we'd love to have Tice and Freeborn stay. They could live with us forever and I'd be happy as a lark, and I know your mother feels the same." He looked at Elizabeth who shared a sad smile with him. "But at this point Tice and Freeborn are not 'runaway slaves,' which implies they've finished running away. Until they get to Canada they are '*running* away slaves' because the chase is not over. These slave catchers, some of them anyway, won't give up—even to trudging all the way up here in the Maine woods. It sounds crazy but it's true."

"It's an obsession with some of them," Elizabeth nodded.

"A satanic obsession," Abel added.

"Satanic?" Tice asked.

"It's from Satan," Abel said. "Who is love? God. Who embodies all the opposite of God? Satan. Hate is in the hearts of these men. This Morgan who's chasing you, Tice, he was born in sin; we all are. But he wasn't born with hatred of black people in his heart. That feeling took root somehow and grew in him. Maybe as a child his parents told horrible stories. Satan is the father of lies and there is no telling what lies Morgan has heard over the years. Maybe he hated someone bigger and stronger than him and since he couldn't beat on them he transferred that hate to slaves who had no power over him."

"Maybe Morgan's jealous of our beautiful black skin," Freeborn said with a chuckle as he ran a hand over his cheek.

Abel smiled. "Maybe, Freeborn. We don't know the circumstances, but we know the sinister result. And we know the source: the dark, evil heart of the enemy of God. Our Lord loves you and loves us all regardless of the color of our skin. But His enemy? He hates everyone—black, white, red or yellow."

"And in this case," Elizabeth said, "he's using one to destroy, or try to destroy, the other. In fact, he's using black people to destroy black people. Untold numbers of Africans are captured by other tribes and sold to slave-traders."

"So's you sayin' I shouldn't hate Morgan?" Tice asked.

"Pray for his soul." The answer came from Caleb.

All eyes turned to him.

"That's what my Sunday school teacher, Mister Roberts, says 'bout people you don't care for."

Caleb held up the skin of a baked potato from his plate. "It's like this here tater." Tice could tell Caleb was proud of himself, feeling like a teacher. "Mom baked this tater and it has a hard skin. Sometimes she mashes a tater and it's mushy. The way this tater turns out depends on how it's treated, what it's exposed to. In the oven, its skin becomes hard. Morgan's skin is hard for some reason.

"But mashed up, the tater's all mushy; no hard skin. That's a Christian for ya'—mushy."

"Yeah, you're mushy," giggled Judah. Ephraim laughed and Caleb, sitting next to him, poked him on the arm.

"Generally speaking, you're right, Caleb," said Abel. "But a lot of us are put in the oven of affliction and we make the right choices about how to respond. Only God knows what Morgan has been through and why he is the way he is, while others who have the same type of experiences turn out to be God-fearing people.

"Whatever drives him," Abel continued, "it's a sin against God and—Tice?"

"Yes-sir?"

"The man who wrote that book you're reading, *The Pilgrim's Progress*, said this: 'Sin is the dare of God's justice, the rape of His mercy, the jeer of His patience, the slight of His power and the contempt of His love."

"But you pray for sinners nevertheless," said Elizabeth, "because God can even turn the hardest of baked potatoes into the mushiest of mashed potatoes."

"Yeah, Mom, look at the apostle Paul," Judah exclaimed. "He was baked, for sure!"

"'N God mashed him?" Ephraim asked.

Everyone laughed.

"Yes, Ephraim, God mashed him." Elizabeth said. "Paul went from imprisoning Christians to being a winner of souls for Christ."

"S'pose that will happen to Morgan?" Tice asked.

"Only God knows, Tice," Elizabeth said. "Only God knows. He knows our hearts better than we do. He gives us every chance to come to Him. He'll stand at the door of Morgan's heart, ready to come in—if invited. If Morgan never opens that door, well—"

"Then he'll burn in hell fire," Judah declared with finality.

For a moment Tice felt sorry for Morgan, then remembered the snarl on the man's lips whenever he prepared to batter Tice or another slave.

•••••

Before the sun rose over the horizon the next morning, Caleb came to the attic and rustled Tice and Freeborn out of their cots. "Hurry, fellas, we gotta get going. Dad just heard. The law's coming here this morning. So we got a long, long ways to go today. I'm driving ya' in the wagon 'cause Dad wants to be here when the law comes. It would look suspicious if he weren't Plus he doesn't want Mom here alone. It'll be you and me for a coupla days, at least. We're skipping a coupla stations to get you as far away as possible."

The whole household gathered in the kitchen to say their goodbyes to Tice and Freeborn. Ephraim hugged Freeborn's massive leg and wailed, "I don't want you to go, Free! Mom—Dad, does Free hafta go?"

Abel softly patted the boy's head. "I'm sorry, son, but, yes. I'm told the sheriff's coming here in a couple of hours. We can't take the chance of Freeborn staying. You know that. He and Tice have to travel all the way to Canada."

Ephraim wailed again and fresh tears ran in rivulets down his cheeks as he reached up his arms for Freeborn to hold him. Freeborn pulled the boy up to his chest. "It'll be all right, Eph. Maybe I can come back and visit, sometime. Maybe. If I can, I will. If I can."

"I love you, Free." Ephraim said it unabashedly and put his little arms around the big man's neck.

"Sun's about to come up," Abel cut in. "Better be on your way."

Abel looked squarely at Caleb. "Remember all that I told you. Be careful. Keep Tice and Freeborn hidden. There's snakes in the woods, remember, and these snakes don't crawl on their bellies."

Caleb nodded. "I understand, Dad. I'll be careful."

"Good. I put grain for the horse in a burlap bag in the wagon."

"And there's this food for all of you which should last several days," Elizabeth said, pointing to a basket and a wooden box on the kitchen table.

"You men have your clothes?" Abel asked.

"Yep," Tice said. "In our backpacks by the door."

"Here's some money if you need it." Abel handed both Tice and Freeborn a little bag the size of a fist and they each pocketed them.

Minutes later, Tice, Freeborn and Caleb were on their way. Beautiful yellow and orange hues filled the eastern sky, a sentinel to the sun hiding over the horizon, as they headed on a rough and rutted road northward.

•••••

It would take four long days to reach their next destination: a small community called Brewer, across Penobscot River from the city of Bangor. Each day they rose before sunrise and got on their way. They stopped to eat lunch from Elizabeth's stash, then climbed back on the wagon and rode until the sun was set and they couldn't see the road. Then they would find a place where they could turn off into a field to have dinner and sleep.

The first night they camped in a field next to a narrow brook. They ate cold chicken breasts and drank hot coffee, heated over a little fire.

"Your Mom's a great cook," Tice said to Caleb.

"The best."

"I mean it. Lots of ladies 'n even servants have cooked meals for me since I 'scaped, but your Mom's the best of the best."

"I'll tell her you said so, Tice. That'll make her smile."

"Yep. Sure beats food at the mines!" Freeborn said, chomping down on his breast of chicken."

Caleb washed the tin dishes and cups in a brook, then handed Tice and Freeborn blankets. He took one himself and spread it on the ground.

"What you doin'?" Tice said.

"I found a nice level spot so this is where I'm sleeping."

"Not me!" Tice exclaimed.

"Why not?"

"I remembered your pappy said snakes were in the woods. Yuck! I hate snakes! 'N I ain't never seen no snake that doesn't crawl. That would be scary."

Freeborn laughed. "Why, Tice, Misser Abel was talkin' 'bout people—people who are *akin to* snakes."

"Yeah, he meant a person who is like a snake, and who was a snake in the Bible?" Caleb asked.

"The devil," Tice said.

"Correct. Go to the head of the class," Caleb joked.

"Head of the class?"

Caleb looked keenly at Tice. "Yes, class. School." He saw no recognition of what he was talking about, so added, "Tice, a school is a building where we go to learn about things. How to read, write, add and subtract. A class is a group of kids, called students, who all meet together in one classroom with a teacher who instructs us. So, if you're the smartest student they say, 'Go to the head of the class.'

"That's what I was saying to you 'cause you figured out what Dad meant by there being snakes in the woods. That's why you and Freeborn have to hide in the wagon every time we pass someone on the road. There's people around who want you caught as well as us who want you free."

"Yeah, I know." Sadness filled Tice's words.

"So, you all right about sleeping on the ground? There's no real snakes, as in those that crawl, that'll bother you up here. That kind's all down South."

Tice's eyebrow rose. He wasn't sure about this declaration.

"I promise."

"You do?"

"Sure do."

"Okay, then." Tice walked to the wagon and pulled out two blankets, tossing one to Freeborn, who belly-laughed at Tice's squeamishness.

"You ain't funny," Tice said.

"I is."

"Ain't."

"Is."

Tice poked his big friend on the arm. "Is."

"Ain't."

"Hah!" Tice said. "You just admitted you ain't. It's settled."

Freeborn frowned. "I'm sleepin' on t'other side of Caleb so's I don't roll over and squash you."

Tice laughed. "Watch out, Caleb. He's dang'rous—a dang'rous man."

A minute later they were all lying on their backs looking up at the star-strewn sky. There wasn't a cloud from horizon to horizon. A half-moon shone high above. Everywhere bright stars shined. Some sparkled like jewels.

"There's the North Star," Freeborn said, pointing.

"Yep. Sure is brighter than all the others, isn't it?" Caleb said.

"Sure is."

"The way I find it is it's so close to the Little Dipper."

"Little Dipper?" Tice asked.

"Yep. You know the dippers you use to drink water out of?"

"Yeah."

"Well, look there. See that dipper?" Caleb pointed to the stars that formed the constellation.

"Yeah. I see!" Tice exclaimed.

"Well, that's how I find the North Star. I look for the Little Dipper first. I don't have Freeborn's natural North Star inclination."

"Inclination?"

The boys spent hours talking about stars and animals and families and freedom and good food and sleeping indoors as opposed to out of doors and getting warm by a fire and swimming in a cool stream on a hot summer's day. And each subject led to God.

The stars led to talk of the star that guided the wise men to the baby Jesus.

The animals led to discussion of how very different they are from one another, and from humans; how dogs are the perfect example of what God wants His people to be: loyal, helpful, true and giving unconditional love.

The talk of families led to the way the Lord wants

all His people to be, sharing what they have in body, soul and spirit; helping those who are poor, hungry, thirsty, in jail; giving to the orphans and widows.

Freedom meant not being a slave to any one or any thing, except God. "Like the apostle Paul," Caleb said. "Somewhere in the Bible he didn't want to go to Jerusalem. Everyone told him bad things would happen to him if he went. But he said, 'I go bound in the Spirit to Jerusalem.' He was doing what God wanted, not himself. He had completely given his will over to God. A willing slave, by choice; not a servant captured and used against his will like you two. And 'cause he and the other disciples were willing slaves, Jesus called them 'friends.'"

When good food came up, Caleb told the story of God providing manna in the desert. "Angels' food," he said.

"Aw!" Tice and Freeborn both responded, licking their lips.

Sleeping indoors? "It's okay as long as there ain't no fleas 'n bugs," said Freeborn.

"Yeah, there may be bugs but there's never no snakes inside," Tice said.

"You and snakes," Caleb ribbed him. "I'm gonna catch a snake tomorrow and we'll tackle that fear of yours, Tice."

"Oh, no."

"Oh, yes."

"I thought you said not to worry 'bout snakes."

"These ones won't hurt you. We haven't got any of those dangerous snakes in Maine."

Getting warm by a fire? "On a cold day, it's the best feelin' in the world—puttin' your hands over the flames makes the heat go through your whole body," Tice said.

"That's what it felt like the day I got filled with the Holy Spirit," Caleb said.

"Yeah?"

"Yeah. I was praying to God, telling Him I loved Him and that I wanted to get closer to Him than bark on a tree. I heard a voice—I think a small voice in my mind—say, 'Raise up your hands.' So I did. And suddenly, whoosh, a heat came through me from my hands down to my head all the way down to my toes. I felt like I was wrapped up in a pile of blankets that had been heated up in an oven."

"Whoa!" said Freeborn.

"Better believe it. Whoa!"

"Did you stay like that? Warm all over?" Tice asked.

"For a minute or two. Long enough to know that God had answered my prayer. Long enough to know it wasn't just my mind playing tricks. Long enough that I'll never forget it. And long enough that I'll forever believe the Lord is right there listening to me, ready to answer, wanting to make me a man of God."

"'N the Holy Spirit does that?" Freeborn's eyes were wide open.

"Sure does."

"Can I get it?"

"Him."

"What?"

"The Holy Spirit's a 'him,' not an 'it,' Freeborn. He's part of God."

"Yeah?"

"Yeah. It's complicated. God, Jesus and the Holy Spirit are all one."

"How?"

"It's hard to fathom. Think of it like water. The same water in here," he pointed to a water jug, "can be steam if put over the fire like that," he pointed to a pot hanging over the fire which was dying down, "and it can also be ice when it gets cold enough. Flowing water, steam, ice—all three are water, like God."

"Awesome." Tice felt a tingle down his spine. "God's even more amazin' than I thought."

"Okay, but how do I get Him?" Freeborn interjected.

"Ask," Caleb said. "Just ask. You don't have to make it complicated. Simple is good. God just wants you to ask. Jesus said when He went away to heaven He would send the Holy Spirit to guide us."

"That'd be better 'n the North Star, even," Freeborn said.

"Sure would."

Sitting right there under the stars, Tice and Freeborn followed Caleb's lead and the Holy Spirit descended on them like a dove.

"I've got the heat," Freeborn said excitedly.

"No heat here," Tice said, "but I do feel a peace. A real deep peace."

They slept a deep and restful slumber, waking up when they heard a rustling in the woods. All three turned on their stomachs to see three whitetail deer—a buck with a big rack of antlers, with a doe and fawn—chewing on apples hanging down from a wild apple tree at the edge of the meadow. The deer didn't notice, or didn't care, that three humans were nearby.

"Look at 'em. Not afraid a bit," Caleb said.

"The little one knows his pappy's there to protect him," Tice said. "Like my Pappy did."

"Like your heavenly Daddy does," Caleb said.

"Right." The thought of a Protector took even deeper root in Tice's heart. "You're right."

•••••

The next morning, the three of them were eating a breakfast of bacon and eggs cooked over a small fire when Caleb suddenly jumped up.

"Be right back," he said and hustled across the meadow.

"What's up with him?" Freeborn asked. All he and Tice could see was Caleb reaching down to the ground.

Tice shrugged.

"He should be a teacher, don't ya' think?"

Tice nodded.

"He could prob'ly teach the Bible."

Tice nodded.

"'N we could learn from him."

Tice nodded. He and Caleb had been reading *The Pilgrim's Progress* aloud in the firelight at night—Tice stammering over a lot of the words but getting better at it all the time. So far, he could sound out most of the words but didn't figure he could write them very well without looking at them. As they progressed in the book, Caleb was leading him and Freeborn to advance toward a better understanding of God.

When Caleb returned, he had a hand behind his back. Reaching Tice and Freeborn, he brought his arm around. Hanging from his hand was a green snake about a foot and a half long. Tice nearly jumped out of his clothes.

Freeborn laughed and rose to his feet. "Tice, you're nearly turnin' white!" he exclaimed.

Tice scuttled backward, nearly tripping over his own feet. "I *is* white," he hollered, "white with fear."

"Tice," Caleb said, "there's no reason to be afraid. That's why I brought this little fella back with me. He's a harmless little garden snake, that's what Dad calls them. He's more scared of you then you are of him. That is, you shouldn't be afraid at all. You're a giant in his eyes. A giant!"

Tice stopped his retreat. "A giant?"

"Yeah, look how little he is. When we're around,

he's afraid we could squash him. And we could."

"But, yuck, Caleb. Yuck! My spine tingles 'n my skin crawls just lookin' at him."

"That's what I want you to overcome, Tice. Look at this snake like you would a bird, or a horse."

"Yeah, oniy it crawls along on its belly," Freeborn giggled.

Tice shot Freeborn a "shut-up" look and Freeborn stopped abruptly.

"Tice," Caleb said, "to this snake you're scary for walking on feet. And the horse is scary because it's got four feet to your two. And the bird's scary because it swoops through the air. We're all different but we shouldn't be scared by the differences. All God's creations show His creativity.

"It's like Dad was talking about when he said Freeborn was really dark, you're not so dark, I'm medium dark, Mom's lily white. So what? Should I be scared of you because you're dark?"

Tice shook his head.

"Are you scared of Mom because she'd make a bed sheet look tanned?"

Tice shook his head and laughed. "No, I'm not scared of your Mom. I loves her."

"Well, there you are, then. And I could grow to love this snake if I had a mind to." Caleb rubbed a finger along the back of the snake's head. I could bring him home with me and feed him bugs and make him a pet."

"Yish!" That came from Freeborn.

"Well, I could." Caleb walked toward Tice. "Now don't go running. Here, take a closer look and try not to flinch or be scared."

Tice hesitated, gauging how far away the wagon was if he decided to run to it.

When Caleb was three feet away from Tice he held up the snake, patting its head as he did. "Now, Tice, pat him on the head, right here."

Tice shook his head.

"Freeborn," Caleb nodded to his friend, "come on over and show Tice this is a good snake. Matter of fact, I'm calling him Jonathan."

"Jonathan?" Freeborn repeated.

"King David's best friend."

"Just like a Chadwick," Tice chuckled. "Another name from the Bible."

Caleb noted that if Tice was light-hearted enough to joke he could progress to the next step. "Come on, Tice, join Freeborn in making Jonathan feel loved."

Tice gingerly stepped forward and put out a hand—to the side of the snake in case it decided to bite him.

"He won't bite," Caleb said. "Pat him right there."

Tice did.

"That's great," Caleb said. "You're overcoming your fear.

Tice nodded.

"Oh, gee, you know what? I didn't finish my breakfast. Can you hold Jonathan for a second?"

Without waiting for a reply, Caleb handed the snake to Tice, then spun around and walked back to the fireside. Before he realized it, Tice was holding the snake just below its head. Suddenly he looked, startled, at Caleb. "But—!"

Caleb turned to look at him. "But?"

"But—"

"I think you've got a new friend, Tice."

Freeborn laughed and put out a hand to pat the snake.

•••••

A half hour later, their blankets and frying pan packed and Tice having let the snake go into the field, they were again on their way.

"Bumpity-bump. Bumpity-bump. Every road we ride on seems bumpier than the last," said Tice, sitting to Caleb's right.

"Be thankful we're not lying down in the back," said Freeborn to Caleb's left.

"Rough, huh?" Caleb said.

"So rough's I'd rather be workin' in the mine during that time. 'Course then I think about 'scapin' and I'd rather suffer while 'scapin' than be a mule in the mine."

"Mule?" Caleb asked.

"Boss thinks I's so big that he should give me all the toughest jobs, so he nicknamed me 'Mule.'"

Caleb shook his head in disgust.

"Mean man," Tice said.

Appearing to eschew sympathy, Freeborn changed the subject. "Railroad's the best way to travel," he said.

"Yeah, if you's can beat the dog to the boxcar," Tice said.

"Dog?" Caleb asked.

"We's lucky on our plantashun," Tice said. "We didn't have dogs trained on us. But some massahs train dogs to the smell of the slaves, so if they try to run away the dog can track 'em. Massah didn't have no dogs to chase after us, but Morgan somehow got hold of one—prob'ly from the man who was with him. Nearly caught me on a train, too."

The thought of that race to the train and hiding in the darkness of the boxcar came back to Tice as fresh as this morning's snake escapade. The big dog's sharp bark, his run—his leap! A chill flew down Tice's back, twittering along his spine all the way.

"Must be vicious dogs." Caleb's remark interrupted Tice's recollection and he breathed a sigh of relief. Right now, he thought, I's free. Right now I's headin' to safety. Right now they's no whip at the hand of Morgan or Massah, no dog a-chasin', no police on t'other side of the bookcase. He breathed deeply—the air of freedom.

Chapter Eight
Hannibal Hamlin!

Two days later they were riding along the west side of a wide river.

"This the same river as last week?" Freeborn asked.

"Nope." Caleb pulled the horse to a stop at the water's edge. "That there was the Androscoggin River. This here's the Penobscot. Up ahead is Bangor, the lumber capital of the world. Ha!" He laughed.

"What's so funny?" Tice asked.

"Dad tells this story about Bangor. It was really supposed to be called Sunbury."

"Yeah?"

"When the settlement grew big enough, the townspeople decided they'd get the place incorporated—"

"In-cor—," Freeborn questioned.

"Well, they weren't formally a town and they wanted to be recognized as one," Caleb answered. "This was back sixty, seventy years ago. Anyhow, so they got together and decided to call it Sunbury, a real pleasant name, right?"

"Right," Tice and Freeborn responded together.

"So they sent Reverend Seth Noble to ask the

Massachusetts General Court to incorporate the town under the name Sunbury. While waiting to petition, the good reverend whistled one of his favorite melodies, a Welsh folk tune called *Bangor*. When the magistrate asked the name of the town, Reverent Noble thought he was asking the name of the tune he was whistling and said, 'Bangor.'

"So," Caleb laughed, "instead of this place being called Sunbury, it's Bangor!"

They all laughed.

"Anyhow, Caleb said, "once we get into Bangor a ways we'll head over a bridge across the river—into Brewer. We cross a bridge, go up a short hill and there's the big house you're staying at next."

"Yeah?" said Tice.

"Well, it isn't any hovel." Caleb straightened up and his eyes lit up. "It's a beautiful home, called the Christmas House 'cause it's all lit up at Christmas. It was built by John Holyoke (God bless his soul), a deacon in the First Congregational Church who died before I was born—probably thirty years ago."

Caleb turned to his two charges. "Dad says there's some pro-slavery folks in this area, so's it's best you both hide under the canvas 'til we get there."

Caleb watched Tice and Freeborn, who didn't hide their reluctance as they took their places in hiding with which they were now familiar.

Caleb snapped the reins and rode on, keeping an eye on the road ahead into the city of Bangor and looking across the river to the smaller community of Brewer Village, where he spotted a gristmill, shingle and clapboard mills, a shipyard—no, two—what appeared to be a mast and spar maker. It was a thriving town, with spinning-wheel and carriage makers, shoe manufacturers, stove and furnace makers and at least two ice companies. Bangor was a lumber port and, with that, came all the vagaries of the trade. With lumberjacks pouring into town, their pockets full of money, bars and brothels were popular, especially along the infamous Exchange Street. That's where Deacon Holyoke had made his fortune—as a lumberyard owner and shipbuilder.

The pungent smells from a tannery wafted toward Caleb. The stench from the process of scraping fat from animal hides to turn them into coats and shoes and other goods was almost overpowering.

"Yuck! What's that?" Tice whined from beneath the canvas.

"Just hold your nose for a while. You'll survive," Caleb joked, scrunching his own nose.

A few minutes later they passed a brickyard, first a soak pit where clay was mixed; then a soft-mud brick-molding machine which apparently wasn't working and had two men working frantically to fix it, one cursing in no uncertain terms at the other to do what he was told; then the brick-drying area where the bricks were left to dry in the sun. Caleb looked up at the blue skies and thought how thankful the brickyard workers must be that rain wasn't in the air. Finally, he passed a large kiln and could nearly feel the heat from its fires.

What a metamorphosis, he thought, to go from clay in the ground to a hard, durable, solid mass—a brick that would become a vital part of a building. Like us, he thought, who believe in God. And he wondered where he was in the process. At his age, he was probably just in the soaking pit.

What about Tice and Freeborn, he wondered. Probably they were just dug out of the ground. Did he and his family have anything to do with their development? He certainly hoped so because, after today, his chance was gone.

He looked to the heavens as he continued on along

the main street of Bangor, hugging the river to his right. Did I share enough, teach enough? he asked silently. *Love, the response came. Showing and sharing your love is always enough. Don't worry.*

Further along was the Muzzy Company, a foundry and machine shop beside the river that turned out sophisticated sawmill and farm machinery as well as stoves and other ironware. His Mom's stove came from here.

What a place! Caleb thought, comparing Bangor to Vassalboro and even Augusta. This is where the King of England used to get masts for his navy's ships.

As they reached deep into the city, Caleb noticed that the traffic was nearly non-existent. *This is odd.* And as he drew about a quarter-mile from the bridge he noticed Concord coaches and carriages tied up alongside the street. Even handcarts were left aside the throughway.

A stagecoach rumbled by and the driver slowed to call down to Caleb from his perch, "No gettin' through there, son. The crowd's filled the street. I barely squeezed through 'em all myself."

"Why's that?" Caleb called back.

"Hannibal Hamlin's speakin'. Looks like everyone in town who's not anchored to an anvil or such is here to listen."

Hannibal Hamlin. Caleb absorbed the information. *Hannibal Hamlin!*

Caleb leaned back over his shoulder. "Tice, Freeborn."

"Yeah," came the muffled reply from underneath the blankets. "Be still but be listening. You gotta hear this. The man I'm praying is the next vice president of the United States of America is speaking up ahead. I'll get the wagon as close as I can so we can all hear him. But be invisible. There's a big crowd."

A minute later Caleb pulled the horses to a stop on the edge of a crowd of hundreds, perhaps thousands. Caleb stood up and scanned the throng. A ripple of excitement ran down his spine. Bangor's own Hannibal Hamlin. Chosen by Abraham Lincoln as his running mate.

Caleb looked intently to where all eyes were turned. There he was: a distinguished-looking, broad-faced man who appeared around 50 years old, standing on a makeshift platform; a farm-raised boy who became a lawyer then rose in politics to the House of Representatives as a Democrat, becoming speaker and then voted into the Senate; a staunchly moral politician who had left the Democrat Party because of its strong pro-slavery stance. And now he was running to be vice president as a Republican. And now Caleb could listen to him! And what might Tice and Freeborn learn?

"You ready to listen?" Caleb asked.

"We's listenin'," Tice and Freeborn replied.

"... even Maryland's eloquent William Pinkney declared that slavery 'scorches the green earth upon which its footsteps fall'!" Hamlin declared.

Caleb pumped his chest out. *Oh, this was going to be good!*

"When our Constitution was formed," Hamlin said, "nobody doubted, everybody expected, that the institution of slavery, so lethal in its effects, would fade away. But times have changed. The invention of the cotton-gin made the production of cotton profitable, and, with that power, public sentiment has changed in the South, and too much here in the North."

Caleb noticed Hamlin's eyes in the distance wandering over the crowd and it appeared his eyes locked on Caleb. It seemed like he was speaking loud enough just so even a teenager on a distant buckboard could hear every word clearly.

"Slavery might help the South temporarily. But permanently? It is a blight!"

Mostly cheers greeted this statement, but Caleb noticed some disgruntled objections.

"In the Convention which framed the Constitution," Hamlin continued, "James Madison told us that it was wrong to admit that man could hold property in man. Madison would not incorporate that idea into the Constitution. We have the maxims and the teachings of Thomas Jefferson and all the wisest and best statesmen of the South against slavery. I have no time to stop now to quote authorities, but they are 'thick as autumnal leaves.'"

Shouts of agreement from the crowd met this declaration, but Caleb noticed that a couple of men standing near his wagon simply crossed their arms and scowled.

"Listen, my friends. We here in the North had no natural advantages like those that God gave the South. But placed as we were, and judging that the fiat of the Almighty was no curse upon man, that he should earn his livelihood in the sweat of his own brow, we have toiled in our forests and on our hillsides; we have forged in our machine shops; we have delved in our mines; and we have made the North, under all the circumstances in which we have been placed, what she is."

Hoorahs greeted Hamlin's praise.

"And we have done all this without slavery!"

More cheers. Still, Caleb observed the two men nearby grumbling between themselves.

"The South holds firm all arms of the government," Hamlin continued, his voice rising. "It seized upon the Executive and bound him in its manacles. It has the Legislative power in its grip. It controls the Judiciary in its grasp. How it got the Judiciary and Congress I do not precisely undertake to say—by political complicity and collusion, anyhow."

Whoa! Caleb thought. That is a damning statement said anywhere, and a dangerous one in some places.

"The High Court?" Hamlin said. "We make laws; they interpret them. But it is not for them to tell us what are the limits within which we shall confine ourselves in our action; or, in other words, what is a political, constitutional right of Congress, any more than it is for us to tell them what is a judicial right that belongs to them. Of all despotisms upon earth, the despotism of a Judiciary is the worst. It is a life estate!"

"No more life terms for judges!" hollered a man on the fringe of the crowd.

Shouts from the crowd agreed.

Hamlin nodded, then raised his hands to quiet the gathering and continued: "Ladies and gentlemen, I speak of the North and the South. But in my heart, I know no North, no South, no East, no West. We are the people of one common country. Whatever relates to the prosperity and the welfare, whatever pertains to the rights of the South, as an American citizen, as an American Senator, I stand here to vindicate and maintain. What are their rights are our rights. What belongs to them belongs to us, as citizens of a common country.

"Mister Lincoln and I are running to be President and Vice President of the United States of America. We regard our country as a whole. We are willing to stand by it as a whole. Nay, in the Union, we mean to stand by it as a whole. You can neither drive us out of it, nor shall you go!"

Around the crowd men raised their hands in agreement.

Caleb noticed Tice and Freeborn squirming to get their heads above the blankets so they might hear more clearly. He looked at the two mean men and fear rushed over him. He quickly whispered to the two slaves, "Careful, fellas."

"You all know," Hamlin continued, "that I was a member of what is called the Democrat Party. I say 'called'—yes, 'called'—and it is a burlesque indeed to speak of that party as democratic. It adopts none of the maxims of democracy, none of the tenets which we suppose belong to a Democratic Party: a free government, a liberal government, in which the rights of the people are to be paramount. No, it does no such thing; and it is therefore a burlesque—a travesty, a mockery!"

Hamlin drew a deep breath. Then he asked: "Friends, what evil has overtaken that Democrat Party's control?"

"Greed!" called a man standing at the foot of the platform. The crowd yelled in agreement.

"Power!" hollered a man in the midst of the throng. Again the crowd agreed in unison.

"Here is an example of the thinking that has led to the sorry state of the heart of the Democrat Party," Hamlin said. "Senator Hammond from South Carolina actually supported his party's stance on slavery by quoting the words of Christ: 'The poor ye will always have with you.'"

Caleb nearly gasped at the idea that a United States senator—actually, any grown person—would so use Jesus' words to defend slavery.

"Well, Christ's statement about 'the poor' is true. There is no denial of the fact," Hamlin called out. "There is, however, another maxim of the same Good Book, which Mister Hammond might have quoted with just as much propriety, and with greater truth: 'Do ye unto others as ye would that others should do unto you, for this is the law and the prophets.'

"Does poverty imply crime?"

"No!" the crowd responded.

"Does poverty imply servitude?"

Again, "No!"

"Does poverty imply slavery?"

"No!"

"The senator is correct: in all climes, in all countries, and in all ages, there are poor. Because men are poor, does that imply that they are to be placed on the same basis with persons who are subjugated, and who toil in the chains of slavery?"

"No!" the clamor rose higher still.

"I also deny it." Hamlin pointed to his chest. "There is a prompting of the heart, there is a principle of Christian benevolence, that tells you, and tells me, and tells us all, that if there are poor, it is our duty to alleviate their poverty, and to remove their distress—not, because they are poor, to class them in the same condition with negro slaves.

"But as the South can not in truth defend slavery by quoting this scripture, neither can we as a nation defend it on any scale. God forbid that we should class the poor with the slave that toils only to live, and lives only to toil. And God forbid slavery of any kind."

Cheers rang out. Caleb jumped up and down and nearly fell out of the wagon, catching himself with his hand on the back of the seat. The two men angry at Hamlin heard Caleb, looked at him and glowered.

"Any man who is an observer of things could hardly pass through our country without being struck with the fact that so much capital, enterprise and intelligence is employed in directing slave labor," Hamlin said. "And one consequence we overlook—that the South so totally is blind to—is that a large portion of our poor white people are wholly neglected, and are suffered to while away an existence in a state but one step in advance of the Indian of the forest.

"Without slavery wouldn't there be work for these people?"

"Yes!" screamed the crowd.

"So, by eliminating one evil we would also correct one problem."

"Yes!"

"Do we not believe that nations, like individuals, must answer to a higher power for the wrongs they perpetrate?" Hamlin asked.

"They must!" cried out a woman. That caught everyone by surprise because women did not usually act so in public. A skittering of mirth spread through the crowd.

"And if we believe that the sins committed by a nation are to be answered for as are the sins of an individual—," Hamlin hesitated, "can we doubt that a fearful retribution must follow if the present course of things continues?"

"No!" The throng was animated now, as if it were one person. Though with a few misguided fingers and toes, Caleb thought as he eyed the two angry men who, incensed, turned abruptly and stomped away toward the bridge on the other side of the crowd.

"Then vote for the ticket," Hamlin said, "of Lincoln and Hamlin!"

Cheers and near delirium ruled the next few minutes as Hamlin descended the staging and walked among the people.

As the edges of the crowd dissipated, the way was made for Caleb to ride toward the bridge. Still tingling from the excitement, he sat down. "Hunker down, guys. We're goin'," he said.

Tice and Freeborn did as they were told.

Caleb snapped the reins and the horse took off, pulling them along behind him.

Within a minute they approached the two men Caleb had identified as slave-haters. They were walking along the right side of the street, talking animatedly. Fear played a game along Caleb's neck. He lifted his left elbow to ninety degrees and whispered hoarsely underneath it, "Be quiet and still, Tice, Freeborn."

Freeborn, not understanding, lifted up the blanket and called, "What's that, Caleb?"

Caleb flinched. The man on the left apparently had noticed the movement in the wagon, which was now beside him.

"Hey, there!" the man called.

"What?" Caleb answered, snapping the reins with fervor.

"Wait up, boy!" The man grabbed for the sidewall of the wagon and got his hand on it.

Urging the horse into a gallop, Caleb replied, "Can't." The man lost his grip as the wagon pulled away.

"We mean it," the other man hollered. "You stop right there, boy. Somethin's fishy."

"Gotta hurry," Caleb called back over his shoulder. "That awful speech held me up too long. I'll be fired from my job!"

Both men started to run at the wagon and were very close. But Caleb pulled a whip out of a holder beside him and lashed at the horse. "Giddyup!" he hollered.

As the men were about to jump on the back of the wagon, it nearly leaped into the air and took off across the bridge from Bangor into Brewer.

"Hold up!" the men called.

"Can't!" Caleb retorted again, hoping against hope that they would not follow, for at the end of the bridge was a hill. He turned to look and the men, angry as they were, had given up their chase.

Phew!

In a moment, as if driven by a higher power, the horse pulled Caleb and the others quickly up the hundred-yard hill without the least bit of problem. Adrenaline was driving the horse as it would a man being chased by the law.

•••••

What Caleb did not notice as he raced over the bridge was the ship The Mohawk cruising up the Penobscot River. Once called The Penobscot, the ship had been renamed The Mohawk and converted to a schooner because the winds along the coast of Maine were strong enough to move a mountain. The Mohawk's long bow pointed to a dock on the Bangor side of the river. The jib sail was limp and the main sail was being slackened as the captain urged the boat alongside the wharf and his crew set to throw large ropes to the tie-up.

Onboard, while most all the passengers were closely watching the docking operations, a single man stood at the bow of the second deck of the three-deck ship. His attention focused elsewhere, to the bridge a quarter-mile away. *Why had those two men chased after that wagon?* Morgan twirled his mustache and wondered.

•••••

Caleb snapped the reins and urged the horses up the incline. "Giddya!" he called. "Giddya!"

At the top of the hill he came to a crossroad and pulled left. Only at that point did he chance a moment to glance back to the bridge to see where the two men were.

Phew! They had not chased after him. *Lazy!*

"Stay down for another minute," Caleb said over his

shoulder. "We're almost there."

With that, he guided the horse a few yards along the northbound road and turned alongside the first home, a large yellow two-story structure. The driveway led straight toward a red barn.

Caleb tied the reins and leaned back toward Tice and Freeborn. "Hold still just a minute, fellas. I'll be right back."

Caleb jumped down from the wagon, skipped up to a door at the back corner of the house and was ready to knock on the door when it opened.

"Young Mister Chadwick!" exclaimed a handsome woman about 40 years old and even a bit taller than Caleb. Obviously by her dress and demeanor, Mildred Holyoke was a person of means, but Caleb knew she treated everyone as equals—everyone.

She looked over his shoulder. "Isn't your father with you?"

"No, ma'am." Caleb suddenly remembered he was wearing his hat and quickly removed it. "I've come alone. There's trouble back home. Slave hunters looking everywhere. So Dad sent me alone to deliver two packages directly to you."

Mildred Holyoke's brow knit at the mention of slave hunters. "You can never be too careful, Caleb. Put your wagon in the barn, but wait until dark before bringing them in. There are prying eyes around here, too, though most all Brewer folks are against slavery for the mere immorality of the cruel institution."

"Yes, ma'am."

"And you, too, stay with us tonight, won't you? Siras is due home from work in a couple of hours. He'll want to visit with you and catch up on the news from Vassalboro and Augusta."

"We're in a rush to get my friends into Canada. Authorities were sniffin' around our house the day we left."

Mildred Holyoke nodded. "Okay, then. Get your friends settled out in the barn. Better stay with them until you all can come in. The hayloft is the best place both to rest and get fresh air. Open up the large window at the back of the loft."

Caleb rode the wagon into the barn. Soon, the horse taken care of, the three of them were sitting on bales of hay in the loft, high above the wagon. They had opened the rear window and were watching the busy city across the river. Tied down on the pier below the bridge was a handsome boa, The Mohawk.

"Wouldn't it be fun to ride up the river on that?" Tice asked.

"Only rich people would be on it," Freeborn said.

"Only white people," Tice added.

"But nice people. All nice folks," Freeborn said.

Tice nodded assent. "Surely, all nice folks out for a nice ride with nothin' on their minds but enjoyin' God's green creation."

•••••

Morgan curled his whip around his forearm, picked up his bag and stepped down the gangplank off the boat. This town would submit to his authority. This town would cringe, cower. No more of this stiff-necked Yankee better-than-thou! His free fingers squeezed the tip of the whip and fingered the steel he had inserted there. He assessed the swirl of people around him.

They had apparently been gathered for something special. Some sort of Yankee tripe, probably, he thought, and his mouth twitched in a growl.

•••••

Feather bed? Oh-h, a f-e-a-t-h-e-r bed. The feel of what Tice was lying on—or, more precisely, in—must be like heaven. They had spent the evening with Siras and Mildred Holyoke and were now in a large bedroom ready for a restful sleep.

"This is like lyin' in a cloud—a big puffy cloud," Tice said into the darkness.

"Or a big ole bag stuffed with air." Freeborn's baritone voice was soft, like he was asleep and enjoying a fine old dream.

"Yeah, and here I am lying on the floor!" Caleb declared, obviously feigne, Tice thought.

"Your choice," Freeborn rebutted, then laughed quietly, but loud enough so as to tickle Caleb. "How'd you say it?" Freeborn raised his voice as much as he could. 'Oh, guys, you're gonna be in the woods for a week or two more 'n I'm goin' home to a nice warm bed. You fellas take the goose down.'"

Tice laughed. "He's got ya' there, Caleb. Got ya' good 'n fine. But you can squeeze in here with me if'n ya' want."

"Squeeze is right," Caleb said. "Naw, I'm all right. Thanks anyhow, Tice."

Suddenly there was a rap on the door and it opened. Mildred Holyoke was holding up a lantern, obviously upset.

"Boys! Boys!" she said. "I'm so sorry. You've got to hurry!"

Stifling a yawn, Tice curled his legs and turned to sit in bed.

"There's little time," Mildred said. Her urgency was palpable. "You've got to go down through the basement and then through the tunnel to the boat launch."

"Tunnel?" Tice said.

"Boat *lunch*?" Freeborn said.

"Boat *launch*. Yes."

"Always thinkin' about food," Tice giggled. "A launch is where they puts in the ferry."

"Well," Mildred said, "in this case it's a canoe."

"What's that?" Freeborn ask.

"You'll see. Just hurry, boys!"

The three jumped up. They already had their pants and socks on and just had to pull on shirts and shoes.

"Mister Holyoke will detain these people at the front door," Mildred said as they tied their shoes. "Caleb will show you down the tunnel. Friends of ours will meet you down at the riverbank and get you upriver and on to Canada.

"I'm sorry we couldn't take better care of you boys."

"S'alright, ma'am," Tice said. "We's unnerstand. We's gotta run. Always gotta run. Run, or train, or wagon. But never been on a boat before."

"No feather bed tonight, either, huh?" Freeborn chuckled, poking Tice on the arm.

"Nope. Guess not." Tice stood.

"This way, guys," Caleb said.

With Mildred rushing ahead of them down the stairs, and Caleb on her heels, Tice and Freeborn hefted their duffle bags and ran after them.

Siras stood at the foot of the stairs. "Hurry, hurry! They're at the edge of the road!"

Mildred, eyes wide, hurried to the back of the house.

Entering into the kitchen, she opened a door, turned and pointed to a torch secured in a holder on the side of a set of stairs. "Caleb, here are some matches. Light this torch and have lightning at your feet."

She looked at Tice and Freeborn, and Tice sensed a strange mixture of fear, sorrow and hope in her face. "Godspeed, Tice." She hugged him, hard, around the neck. "And to you, too, Freeborn. The Lord be with you."

Freeborn towered too high above her for her to hug him, so she squeezed his arm. "Now, hurry!"

In a moment, Caleb had the torch lit and the three boys raced down the stairs, Caleb in the lead, followed by Tice and then Freeborn.

After a dozen or so steps, they came to the basement.

"This way, guys!" Caleb stepped quickly to a rack of flowers hanging to dry and pushed it to the side. Beneath, on the floor, was a metal hook. Caleb handed the torch to Tice, then squatted and grabbed hold of the hook. With a heave, he pulled up a round slab of wood about four inches thick and a foot-and-a-half in diameter. Caleb reached up, motioning for Tice to hand him the torch.

"There's a ladder that takes us down a few steps to a tunnel," Caleb said. "Freeborn?"

"Yeah."

"Pull that slab back into the hole after you step down to the ladder, okay?"

"Gotcha."

Before Tice noticed, Caleb disappeared into the black hole, the light from the torch first brightening the hole, then the light dimming as Caleb went down the ladder.

"Hurry, Tice!" Caleb called.

Seconds later, Tice and Freeborn joined Caleb in a dark, dank tunnel about four feet wide.

"Stone steps will take us down to the river," Caleb said. "Let's go."

Down and down they went. Tice heard dripping water which landed on the steps with a dim echo. He shivered.

Just as Caleb called, "Watch your footing," Tice slipped on a wet step and fell backwards. His duffel bag hit the stone with a smack.

"Ouch!" he cried. "My arm!"

Caleb turned and came back a couple of steps to where Tice lay, clutching his forearm and wincing.

"I think I broke it!" Tice wailed in pain.

"We can't stop now," Caleb said. "We just can't, Tice."

Tice grimaced and pushed himself up with his good arm.

"Hand me the bag," Freeborn said.

"No, I'll take it," Caleb said and grabbed the satchel. "Let's go."

A memory of falling on a rock in the fields when he was a child picking cotton flashed through Tice's mind. Morgan had walked up to the crying child, yanked him to his feet and kicked his bottom with a gruff, "Stop yer wimperin', boy! Back to work! Animals don't hurt."

A new flood of determination filled him as Tice stood straight and dashed after Caleb. Down and down.

The coolness of the tunnel felt good on Tice's aching arm. Down and down.

Finally they came to an old, worn, wooden door.

Caleb handed Tice the torch and switched the duffle bag from his right shoulder to his left. He pushed down a latch on the door and shoved his shoulder into the door. It creaked open and the boys looked out through a tangle of vines that hung down from above as camouflage.

"Oh, no!" Caleb cried and turned. "The torch, Tice. Give me the torch. We've got to put it out."

Tice handed Caleb the big stick and Caleb smothered the flame in a bucket of water inside the tunnel door.

"Phew! Hopefully no one saw it." Caleb took a step forward and pushed his way through the vines. Tice, forgetting his arm as adrenaline poured through his veins, stumbled after him, with Freeborn in the rear.

A half moon shone dim light on the scene. Before them were shades of darkest black, black and almost black. They were only a few feet from the Penobscot River. A tidal river, its water was flowing inland at the time. The bridge they had ridden over from Bangor to Brewer loomed above them just fifty yards or so downriver.

"Over here." A voice with an odd lilt called from the river out of the darkness.

"Who's that?" Caleb asked.

A breeze along the shore muffled the words, but it sounded like "Clancy and Mac."

"Your Irish and Scottish connection, laddie," came another, rougher voice. "No time to lallygag. But watch yer step. Better to be nimble 'n alive than quick 'n dead."

"Dead." The word landed with a thud in Tice's stomach.

Caleb led the way, covering the distance to the river in a couple of strides.

In the darkness Tice tried to focus on where he was stepping, afraid of falling again and landing on his arm, which was throbbing.

Freeborn stepped past him and handed his backpack to a dim figure standing next to a canoe that rolled slightly up and down in the water. Then Freeborn turned and extended a hand to help Tice over the rocks.

"Who goes there?" A voice from the bridge suddenly called down to them.

Tice, Freeborn and the others looked up to the bridge. A man standing at the railing held out a lantern.

"I think it's one of the men who chased us to the bridge," Caleb said in a low tone.

"Wait there!" the man called.

"Quickly, lads," said Mac, who was seated at the

back of the wide eighteen-foot-long canoe. "Into the boat and into it this moment!"

"Everyone in and I'll push it off," said Clancy. He was standing on the shore holding a rope tethered to the canoe.

"You'll do no such thing!" Tice froze at the sound of that voice. It was Morgan. Morgan!

"You'll hand my boss's property over to me!"

The devil that haunted Tice's dreams stepped out of the darkness, the handle of his whip in his right hand and the thong, fall and popper folded in his left.

Freeborn grabbed Tice by the shoulders and nearly tossed him into the canoe. "Ouch!" Again Tice landed on that arm.

Caleb took a step toward Morgan but the big man simply slugged him on the head with the whip handle, sending him unconscious to the riverbed.

"Be off!" Clancy yelled and began to push the canoe away from shore.

"Wait up there!" came a cry from the man on the bridge. He was now running to the Brewer side.

"Stay where you are," Morgan demanded. "The law's at the front door of the house right now. Probably on their way down here."

"Be off, I say," Clancy shrieked. "I'll take care of this man."

Morgan rushed Clancy and drove the handle of the whip into his stomach, taking his breath away and sending him to his knees, river water washing upon his legs.

Mac paddled backwards quickly, but the canoe's length and weight made it slow to respond. With Caleb and Clancy both on the ground and moaning, Morgan stepped into the water and reached for Tice, who lay in the hull by the bow.

He got hold of Tice's pant leg and was starting to

tug when, seemingly out of nowhere, a large black hand seized Morgan from behind by the collar of his coat, pulled him clear out of the water and tossed him like a bale of hay to the ground.

Tice had struggled to a sitting position and strained to see what was happening. His eyes had adjusted to the darkness enough to see Freeborn looming nearby. "Freeborn, come on!" he urged. "Jump in!"

"You go, Tice. I got a matter to take care of." Freeborn turned to Morgan a moment too late to see the bullwhip snap around his left ankle. With a tug from Morgan, Freeborn fell to the ground and landed on a large boulder.

Tice thought Freeborn might have cracked his head open on the stone. "No!" he cried.

Morgan struggled to his feet and scrambled to the river's edge. He snapped the whip and it whistled toward Tice. It missed him but snaked around the webbing on the stern seat. With a giant tug, Morgan was able to turn the canoe a good ten degrees, the bow turning toward shore.

Mac put his full weight into paddling backward, fighting to resist the pull. It seemed an even battle for several moments, then the canoe began to right itself and Tice felt the help of the incoming current. But, just as suddenly, the canoe jerked again. The man from the bridge had stepped up beside Morgan and added his brawn to the brawl.

The two men tugging on shore against the one man paddling in the canoe was no match. Tice saw a paddle on the floor of the canoe, picked it up with his good hand and tried to help but he felt useless. Morgan grabbed the taut bullwhip and pulled it toward him like in a tug-of-war match. Then the man beside him pulled another length. With each tug the canoe moved closer to shore. The canoe was now within a couple of feet of shore.

Tice hollered, he didn't know what, just hollered. He could see his dream before him—his dream of freedom—disappearing, like so much smoke, into the air. Tears flowed profusely down his cheeks. He screamed again as in torture. He was Morgan's, for sure. He was Massah's. He was property, that's all, no matter who helped him escape, no matter how far he ran, no matter what, just no matter.

Then Tice's eyes widened as he looked behind Morgan. What he saw was fuzzy since he watched through tears, even when he tried to wipe them away. Clancy had risen to his feet and was bent at the waist, apparently catching his breath. With one quick lunge, Clancy grabbed Morgan's cohort by the knees. The man fell to the ground and they began wrestling. Over and over they rolled until they were both half in the river and half out, next to Caleb, still unconscious. At another time of the day a swift current would have pulled them all either toward the ocean or inland.

But Morgan was determined not to let that tussle stop him from his quest.

"I'm gonna get ya', ya' little blackie!" he hollered, then swore a litany of dark oaths. Tice heard each one, taking special note of Morgan's promise to cut out his tongue and feed it to the hogs.

No more prayin' out loud, Tice thought ruefully.

As despair attacked Tice, out of the dark sprang a mammoth figure. Blacker than the blackness of the night. Bigger than Massah's horse. The most welcome sight in Tice's short life. Freeborn!

A shriek flew from Freeborn's mouth that would have scared a ghost and he landed a double-armed blow to the broad shoulders of the slave hunter. Morgan crumbled to his knees.

"Laddie!" Mac called to Tice. "Take this and cut the

whip!" He lobbed a small knife toward Tice. Landing point-down in the canoe. Tice grabbed it, then leaned forward and quickly cut the tip of the whip.

"No!" Morgan howled as he noticed the whip slacken.

"Yes!" Tice responded. "Freeborn, jump in. Jump in!"

Mac had spotted two policemen pushing through the bushes to get to the shoreline and was paddling with abandon. Now the canoe was leaving shore, more quickly.

Unaware of the police, Freeborn wrapped his massive arms around Morgan's chest and squeezed. "Gotta end this, Tice," he called. "You go on. I'll catch up."

Free's gonna crush that man's chest, Tice thought, like a big steel contrapshun. He won't be able to breath. He'll pass out. Maybe he'll die. Maybe.

The police sprung to the scene. "Stop right there, mister," one demanded.

Freeborn simply shook his head.

"Right now!" the other officer insisted, "or I'll use this billy club."

That was the last Tice saw as the canoe pulled away, helped by a current that ran down the center of the river.

Chapter Nine
Up the Penobscot

After escaping off the shore in Brewer with Freeborn bear-hugging Morgan and holding off the police, Mac paddled the next couple of hours. Tice cried through it all—from both pain and emotions.

At one point Tice tried to find the North Star but cloud cover made it impossible. Only shafts of light shone through the clouds from a half moon, just enough to glimmer on the water and show the way north.

Tice could now tell Mac was as short and broad as Clancy appeared tall and rail-thin. Must be as strong as an ox to keep on paddlin', paddlin' paddlin', he thought.

"Tice, laddie," Mac said during a lull in the young man's moaning, "take heart, son. You don't know the news is bad for your friend, or for mine. God's good, son, He's always good. Even when things look in despair, He's good. He'll care for His children when dark gets darker and evil sprouts heads like Medusa's."

"Who's that?"

"Never mind, laddie. Just know that the good Lord is in charge here on His green earth, even when evil raises its homely mug. Like those slave-huntin' goons and others who would make ya' return to yer drudgery.

"Here's me plan." Mac stopped paddling for a moment and leaned toward Tice. "There's an Indian I ken up here in Old Town. I'm going to leave you with him while I go back and get Clancy and see about yer friend."

Mac's accent was unlike any Tice had ever heard. Tice liked the way he spoke, the way words slipped out of his mouth with strange daring. Like his friend Clancy's but rougher and more difficult to understand.

But Tice understood this: he could trust this man with his life. He took comfort in that. His eyes beamed. He smiled broadly. He wiped his nose on his sleeve and looked keenly at Mac. The sun was rising to their right.

"I pray to the Lord they're not in prison, 'n that yer friend's not bein' taken back south. The law says he must be returned to his owner."

Tice nodded and bit his lip, recalling the hard life in the mines that Freeborn had described.

Mac maneuvered the canoe to the shore and they stepped off onto dry land. The older man pulled bread and cheese from a pack and they ate well.

Finally Tice said, "You talk different."

Mac laughed. "Well, I'm not from these parts. I'm from the other side of the ocean, a place called Scotland."

"Yeah?"

"Right-o, laddie. Jolly auld Scotland, a land of marvels and beauty—and poverty that'd make ya' weep." Mac lowered his eyes and shook his head. "That's why I'm here—the poverty."

"Yeah?"

"Fourteen years ago, in the year of our Lord eighteen hundred and forty-six, I was a crofter in Scotland, growing tatties on land belonging to John Gordon of Cluny."

"Tatties?"

"Potatoes, you call 'em." Mac hesitated and Tice could see him recalling his old home with a winsome look.

"Well," Mac picked up, "it wasn't a big plot of land, but enough to feed me, my wifie 'n wee lassie. But, oh, what a year befell us! It was just one year after the Irish tattie famine that drove my friend Clancy Findlen from Ireland to America."

"Yeah?" Tice was intrigued.

"Yeah, indeed. But with Scotland, it was a disease that did us in. Fungal disease, they called it. Destroyed the tatties. Made 'em uneatable. None of us crofters could pay our rent and Mister Gordon, the owner of the land, kicked us oot of our homes. For us, we ended up livin' on the streets of Inverness.

"After a bit 'o time, Mister Gordon—who I think couldn't live with himself for puttin' so many people out 'o their homes—rented a fleet of ships and sailed us tenants to Canada." Mac laughed. "I don't think the government of Canada was too excited about it!"

"Yeah?"

"Yeah. But I wasn't about to accept any handouts. I took me wifie 'n wee bairn and traveled to Maine and found us a bonny property on a burn to grow tatties the likes of which you've never tasted.

"I et my first potato after I 'scaped." Tice smiled. "Had sev'r'l since. I love 'em."

Suddenly Tice turned serious. "Mac," he said, "whys you helpin' me, anyhow?"

"I ken what it's like to be another man's slave, Tice, and I ken what it's like to be free. I despise the former 'n love the latter, 'n that's what I wish for ev'ry man.

"But the better answer is found in the Good Book, where it says, 'For all of you who were baptized into Christ have clothed yourselves with Christ. There's no

Jew nor Greek, there's neither slave nor free man, there's neither male nor female; for you're all one in Christ Jesus.'"

"Not slave or free," Tice repeated, pondering.

A few minutes later, Mac stood up. "My Indian friend lives nearby."

The Scotsman stepped to the canoe and pulled it far away from the water's edge, then shouldered Tice's backpack.

"I sure wish I could help ya'," Tice offered, "but I do think I's broke my arm. It sure hurts awful."

"While I'm gone my friend'll fix ya up better'n any doctor could. You'll be tossin' the caber better'n anyone."

"Caber?"

"Never mind." Mac smiled. "You'll be fixed up's what matters, laddie. Besides, prayin' for our friends back there in Brewer is the best 'work' you can be doin'.

"A couple years ago the other farmers around elected Clancy 'n me to be their go-betweens with the tattie buyers here in the big city. While we're gone they tend to me fam'ly and fields. 'N ev'ry time we come here we check with the Holyokes t' see if there's a slave seekin' freedom that we can help along their way."

As shades of pink that had spread across the sky turned to blue, Tice thought this new day was another miracle. Here he stood and he wasn't workin' in Massah's fields.

•••••

A couple minutes later, they came to a clearing in the woods. A large garden lay before them with all sorts of plants Tice had never seen before and with fruit trees along the edges.

Mac stepped forward and walked down one row of the garden, straight to a two-story home at the far side, a white house with blinds that looked like it belonged in a New England village. After two knocks on the door, it opened wide. A stoutly built man Tice guessed to be forty years old smiled broadly. "Mac!"

"Joe." Mac dropped Tice's backpack to the floor and hugged the man.

"This is my friend, Tice," Mac said.

"Glad to meet you." Joe opened the door wide. "Come in. Come in."

They all stepped inside the cabin. A great room spread before them with beautiful furniture, a living room, dining room and kitchen all in one. At the back, stairs led up to a second floor.

Tice looked intensely at the Indian. He wasn't white and he wasn't black. His hair was long and tied in back. He wore clothing of leather from head to foot. He was a new one on Tice. Finally Tice asked, "Did Mac say your name was Joe?"

"Still is. Why."

"Is we in Old Town?"

"Yes."

"Is your name Joe Polis?"

Joe nodded, wondering how the boy knew his name.

"Do you know a Misser Thoreau from 'chusetts? They call him 'Judge'?"

Joe's face lit up in recognition. "Sure do!"

"Wells, I knows him, too. And he mentioned you to me, said you were among the friendliest people anywhere." Tice smiled at the recollection of the man who talked to him about God, though he had some strange ideas about Him.

"He did, did he?"

"Yeah."

"And when did you meet Mister Thoreau?"

"He helped me 'scape north from there 'n we talked 'bout God."

"That would be right, knowing Judge."

"Why do they call him Judge?" Max asked.

"He's so somber, quiet, doesn't smile much."

"He smiled at me." Tice showed all his teeth.

"I bet he did!"

"'N before I left, he says to me, 'Tice, love your life whether you's rich or poor. Find your life in the livin' of it.'"

Joe weighed the words. "That's Judge all right."

Suddenly Tice winced. A sharp pain shot through his arm.

"What is it?" Joe asked.

"I think he broke his arm, Joe," Mac said. "Can you fix him up?"

"I'll take a look."

Joe proceeded to strap a splint onto Tice's arm that both immobilized it and would make the bone mend correctly.

"You'll be a one-armed man for awhile," Joe said.

"How long?"

"Until you get to Canada anyway."

"How far's Can'da?"

"Far? I don't know miles, but I can tell you travel time," Joe said. "Fourteen days of good travel and you'll be free."

Free. Tice took a deep breath and wondered what freedom felt like. Then his friend's face appeared before him and "Freeborn!" flew from his mouth.

●●●●●

A few minutes later, over a breakfast of bacon, eggs, coffee and milk and biscuits, Mac told Joe about the problems that befell them in Brewer.

"I've got to go back and get Clancy," he said.

"'N Freeborn," Tice added.

Mac shook his head. "I'm sorry, Tice, but I think the law has your friend and, if so, that's that."

"That's that?"

"That's the end of his escape."

All the weeping Tice had done in the canoe had not quite emptied him and he shed more tears.

Mac leaned across the table and put a hand on Tice's shoulder, realizing he should offer hope even if it appeared faint. "It's not a lost cause yet, laddie. Keep yer faith. I'm sure everybody's doin' all they can do—Mister Holyoke especially."

Mac stood to go. "Thanks for breakfast, my friend," he said to Joe. "Can you watch over Tice 'til I return?"

"Of course. Tice and I will enjoy each other's company. I even may show him how to fish. Have you fished before, Tice?"

"Nope." Tice recalled Davey at the big river and talking about fishing.

"Had fun racin' boats, though."

"Boats?"

"Well, sticks we threw in the river."

Mac smiled then turned solemn. "Joe, if somethin' bad happens and I don't return, can you get Tice north to Fort Fairfield?"

Joe nodded.

"To Joseph Wingate Haines' house?"

Joe nodded. "And let Clancy's and my families know?"

"Of course."

"Well, then, laddies, I'm on me way."

Joe and Tice followed Mac to the door and watched him leave. Outside, two white men had arrived and were hard at work in the garden with long wooden-handled utensils Tice was familiar with: hoes. Tice flashed back to Lykins' plantation. No white men hoed the fields there.

A questioning look filled Tice's face and he turned to Joe. "Slaves?"

"Slaves?" Joe repeated, astonished. "No, Tice. Employees. They work for me and I pay them. When we harvest the garden I sell much of the vegetables. My earnings help pay their wages."

Tice nodded. "White men?"

Joe simply nodded assent.

•••••

The next three days Tice's mind was flooded with questions. What could be keepin' Mac? How awful must Freeborn feel, bein' so close to freedom and now goin' back to slavery? Was Caleb okay? What happened to Clancy, anyhow? Was the law now puttin' Mac behind bars, too?

Despite the torture of concern for Freeborn, time passed quickly as Joe introduced Tice to tracking deer and moose, to spearing fish in the moonlight, to discerning what mushrooms and wildflowers he could safely eat. They took excursions in the mornings and afternoons, returning for meals and hoping to find Mac and the others there.

The evening of the third day, Joe said to Tice after dinner, "Pack your knapsack tonight. In the morning we leave for Fort Fairfield."

"But Mac—Freeborn," Tice objected.

"Something's wrong, Tice, or they'd be back by now."

Tice's heart sank. First he lost Freeborn and now Mac as well. And Clancy. And Caleb, too. Caleb was there at the river. What happened to him? Would Tice ever know?

Tice tossed and turned through the night, dark dreams haunting him. In one, he sluggishly tried to run, as if through mud, when a bullwhip snapped near his ear and when he looked in that direction a skull peered at him with a sneer, and he awoke with a scream.

The smell of bacon frying gladly woke him to a fuzzy dusk.

"Didn't sleep well, huh?" Joe said as Tice walked into the kitchen portion of the home's great room, his backpack slung over his shoulder.

Tice shook his head. "Bad, bad dreams."

"Well, you have plenty of good dreams ahead of you—if we can get you out of here. Your day will come, Tice, no doubt."

Joe pointed out a large window on the east side of the house. "Look there."

Tice nodded. "Yeah."

"It's dusk. Barely a candle of light."

"Yeah."

"There're clouds in the sky you can't see. But before long, the sun he will rise and those clouds will make the sunrise more beautiful by far than if no clouds."

Tice pictured billowing pillows of pinks and reds and yellows.

"Think of those clouds as the hard times in your life, Tice."

"Yeah?"

"The day you reach freedom will be much more beautiful because of what you've overcome to get there then if you simply needed to walk off the plantation."

Tice frowned and thought of it: the tiring, long road, the bumpity rides, the clanking trains, the sleepless nights, the constant fear of the chase.

"Things often do not happen when we want, but like

the sun he rise, the Great Spirit his time is perfect for our lives," Joe said.

Chapter Ten
Freedom Awaits

With venison, which Tice declared was his new favorite food, and eggs in their bellies, Joe and Tice left the house packed for a long trip. Joe tacked a note to his door for his workers and carried a satchel of food, Tice his backpack over his right shoulder. His left arm was close to his body in a splint. He hadn't even been able to cut his own venison and felt only half helpful.

Joe stopped and turned to Tice to look him in the eyes. "I do not know what is happening with Mac and Clancy and your friends Freeborn or Caleb, but I do know what will happen to you," he said. "A free man you will be—if I have anything to do with it."

The determined look in Joe's eyes assured Tice, but the anxiety about his friends clung to him like burdocks. It darkened his soul as they walked the trail to the Penobscot River. By the time they reached the riverbank the eastern sky had begun to lighten.

As they drew near, Tice could hear the water flowing. "Here," Joe said, stopping. He stepped into the woods and pulled branches away from a hidden canoe. They put their sacks in the canoe and walked it to the river where Tice stepped into the front and Joe pushed the canoe off into the water, easily sliding onto the rear cane seat and picked up a paddle at his feet.

"Oh, Great Spirit, guide us," Joe said quietly. "Protect us from evil."

Tice took a paddle in his one good hand, determined to help as best he could. He looked toward Brewer. He couldn't see far because of a bend in the river. He did spot the snap of a fish taking a bug off the top of the water for an early breakfast. Nothing more. He lowered his head and wiped away a tear. Big ole Freeborn, he thought. No goodbye to Caleb. No friendly face of Mac. And what about Clancy, 'nother in the long chain 'o people who put their lives on hold 'n in danger to help him, just a slave?

For a few moments Tice was lost in the thought of it as, slowly, they pulled away: Away from Joe's place; from Old Town; from Brewer; from the Chadwicks, Davey, Misser Thoreau, the Balls and Jacksons and funny Bob; from the Randoafs and Miss Weiss; from the plantashun. Headin' toward Can'da—Freedom-land.

Suddenly he heard something different. A screech. An eagle? he wondered, remembering the beautiful large, white-headed bird Joe and he had seen the day before. He looked back over his shoulder, past Joe, in the direction of the screech and scanned the sky, still lightening up but the sun had not risen over the treetops.

No bird but he heard the screech again.

"Look!" Joe said, pointing downstream. "Look, Tice!"

The silhouette of a canoe rounded the bend, heading toward them. Tice put his paddle in his lap, turned in his seat and squinted.

Another screech. Joe laughed. "Let's pull to the shore," he said.

Tice followed Joe's direction and the closer they got to the shore the clearer the silhouette became. There at the front of a canoe was Clancy. At the back of the canoe, Mac. And—between them both—was it? Yes!

Freeborn! Tice nearly jumped out of the canoe in happiness, tipping it wildly. Placing a hand on each side of the bow, Joe got serious very quickly. "Tice! Control yourself!"

•••••

Five minutes later, both canoes had been taken ashore. Handshakes, hugs, laughter—and tears—filled the forest glade where they stood.

"So those bobbies at the door," Clancy said, "were headed to the Holyokes to help Morgan, but on the way headquarters informed them about a fight Morgan had started in the pub. So, knowing where Morgan was heading, they went there to arrest him, not to capture Freeborn and Tice. They saw Morgan headin' to the Holyoke house and followed. It seems Morgan, the big toad, and two other slave-haters he found, had walked into a pub lookin' for help in findin' our friends and, not findin' any assistance, Morgan took to beatin' a man silly, so silly he lies in the hospital one foot in the grave.

"This mornin' Morgan sits in the jailhouse waitin' to see if he faces charges of assault or cold-blooded murder. Either way, he'll not be a problem to our two friends."

"And his two cronies?" Joe asked.

"They sit with him—on charges of aidin' and abettin' a crime."

"But how did Freeborn get free?" Tice asked.

"Our friends, the bobbies, didn't care a wit 'bout Freeborn," Clancy said.

"One of 'em actually pushed me into the shadows and shushed me," Freeborn said, a wide smile crossing his face.

Clancy's eyebrow raised. "Really, lad?"

Freeborn nodded his head.

"Caleb," Tice said. "What about Caleb?"

"Oh, I picks him up outta the river," Freeborn laughed. "He was a big wet rag, sure was. Matter o' fact, he wanted me to give you this here paper." Freeborn pulled a piece of parchment from a pocket and handed it to Tice.

"Dear Tice," Tice read, then handed it to Mac to read aloud.

"Can't," Mac said and pointed to Joe, who took the letter and read:

"I hope some day we will meet again. It has been a privilege being your friend. We are the best kind of friend, you know, the kind that time and place can not separate; the kind God puts together so that no one, not even Satan, can pull apart; the kind that even if we don't see each other again on this earth can look forward with expectation to heaven. I hope my mansion there will be next to yours!

"Read page 263 of 'The Pilgrim's Progress,' where I highlighted it one night when we were camping on the road to Brewer.

"Goodbye, my friend.

"Godspeed, Caleb."

Tice scrambled to pull his copy of the book from his backpack. He handed it to Joe, who took the book and read:

" ' "What must we do in the holy place?" asked the Pilgrim.

" ' The answer came, 'You must there receive the comforts of all your toil and have joy for all your sorrow; you must reap what you have sown, even the fruit of all your prayers and tears and sufferings for the King throughout your pilgrimage. In that place you must wear crowns of gold, and enjoy the perpetual sight and vision of the Holy One, for "there you shall see Him as He is." There also you shall serve Him continually with praise, with shouting and thanksgiving, Whom you desired to serve in the world, though with much difficulty, because of the infirmity of your flesh.

"There your eyes shall be delighted with seeing and your ears with hearing the pleasant voice of the Mighty One. There you shall enjoy your friends again that have gone on before you. And there you shall with joy receive everyone who follows into the holy place after you. There also shall you be clothed with glory and majesty and put into a chariot fit to ride out with the King of Glory.

"When He shall come with a sound of trumpet in the clouds, as upon the wings of the wind, you will come with Him. When he shall sit on the throne of judgment, you shall sit by Him. Yes, and when he shall pass sentence upon all the workers of iniquity, let them be angels or men, you also shall have a voice in that judgment, because they were His and your enemies. Also, when He shall again return to the City, you shall go, too, with sound of trumpet, and be ever with Him.""

Joe closed the book and handed it to Tice. "Mighty good promises."

Tice flashed a jubilant smile that came from a comprehension far beyond his learning.

"Yeah."

END

True North: Tice's Story is a prequel to Mark Alan Leslie's *The Last Aliyah*, which follows descendants of Tice and Caleb Chadwick as they undertake a modern-day Underground Railroad to help Jews escape America when the United States and most of the world impose a law forbidding emigration to Israel.

Read the first chapter of *The Last Aliyah* here, then watch for the release of this exciting new novel.

The Last Aliyah
A Novel
By Mark Alan Leslie

Chapter One

Giant red eyes hovered above and behind Omri Zohn, seeking him out in the moonless night. He hunched down his shoulders to make himself smaller, but knew those eyes were all-seeing—and dreadful. Adrenaline pumped energy through his veins, but it seemed like he was running through deep sand. He could feel sweat behind his ears, an aching right calf— and raw terror.

He reached the crest of a hill, heaved himself forward and landed on the ground. Suddenly a hissing sound, like a wild cat, split the silence; then a snarl, like a mountain lion, caused the hair on his neck to rise. The only sounds: his breathing and the death threat emanating from the supernatural creature.

He pushed himself off the ground and raced down the back side of the hill. He turned to look over his shoulder and the giant eyes rose up over the hill only twenty feet or so behind and ten feet high. Omri knew his remaining moments in this world were numbered unless… unless a miracle…

A sudden high-pitched jangle shattered the night sky—and the dream.

Omri shuddered, half relieved it was a dream and half afraid it was a portent. The jangle was his bedside telephone. He rubbed his eyes and looked at the number calling. 202 area code. His friend, U.S. Senator Joseph Frank. He checked the clok on his nightstand. 3:00. Of course, the hour so many distasteful acts are perpetrated in Washington, D.C.

"Omri! It's Joseph." The voice was tense, urgent and caused Zohn to sit up in his bed.

"They've done it, Omri." Frank's hoarse utterance quaked between a rasp and a gasp. "Congress just approved enforcing the United Nations Resolution."

At those words, Zohn felt an immediate heaviness, as if the darkness in the room had become a physical cloak. The giant red eyes of oppression.

"Five million American Jews and millions of others around the world are now essentially prisoners in our own countries," Frank said. "We're not allowed to go to Israel or any country that defies the UN Resolution outlawing emigration to the Holy Land. Get your escape plan in motion, now, as I will mine."

"Even *you* can't leave?"

"Even I. If it weren't for your classified government work, you might be able to leave because of your dual Israeli-American citizenship. But—" Frank left the sentence unsaid.

"Are there no exceptions, Joseph? My brother, Ariel, just called me yesterday. He discovered he has stage-four cancer and I can't get permission to visit him?" Omri gritted his teeth. "Plus you know that my son and his wife and child moved to Israel a year ago. Can I never be reunited with them?"

"Not a chance—for either reason," Joseph said, "unless Benjamin and his family come back to America. But if they did then, of course, they couldn't be allowed back out of the country. Not unless they've obtained their Israeli citizenship already. Have they?

"No. Not yet. It's a long process."

"I know."

"Can we get out this morning and beat the ban?" Zohn asked.

"Afraid not. The order's immediate. Homeland Security had representatives in the chambers, sitting on the edge of their seats, waiting to give the go signal to headquarters." Frank coughed out a rueful snicker. "Making it more repulsive is that today is August second, the last day before the six-week summer recess. So my colleagues—the brave sort that they are—can vanish into the countryside and avoid any nasty or nagging questions."

A pause, then Frank added, "God speed, my friend! Hopefully we'll meet again in Israel. Shalom."

The line clicked off.

Omri carefully set the phone in its cradle, like he was handling a grenade, and rubbed his eyes. He peered at his bedside clock. It was 3:01. Appropriate, he thought, recalling that Psalm 3 verse 1 reads: "O, Lord, how many are my foes! How many rise up against me!"

He spoke softly the seventh and eighth verses: "Arise, O Lord! Deliver me, O my God! Strike all my enemies on the jaw; break the teeth of the wicked. From the Lord comes deliverance. May Your blessing be on Your people."

He took a moment to reassure himself that the plan he had in place was truly the course of action he wanted to take. His dead wife and daughter were buried in

Israel, having been killed by a terrorist bomb at a bar mitzvah celebration for their nephew a dozen years ago. His boyhood home was there. Besides Benjamin and his new family, Ariel and his family, many cousins and friends lived there. And this ban would prevent him from ever seeing them again, ever paying respects to his wife and daughter, ever setting his feet in the Old City, ever praying at the Western Wall. Besides all that, Israel was the only country in which the Jews could defend themselves.

Omri stiffened his back with determination, swung his feet out of the bed and planted them on the small sheepskin on the wooden floor. He flicked on his bedside lamp. The time has come, he thought. *This will be the last* aliyah, *the final return of Your people to their homeland, Lord. If we can get there.*

•••••

Senator Frank's call to Omri Zohn was just one of a flood of calls, tweets and e-mails in and out of Washington even though daybreak was still three hours away.

Vice President Daniel Fireside could barely contain his excitement. The source of his elation: he had proven that he could indeed push measures through a stubborn Congress—and this particular legislation was the most contentious in his twenty-two years in this contentious Congress in this contentious town, the hub of what had become a contentious country. While he had needed to merely cajole many colleagues into his way of thinking, he had to sternly bludgeon others with substantial threats before they succumbed.

It was astonishing how much you could accomplish by threatening the loss of a coveted committee chairmanship, or removal of a major Naval contract from a person's district. It was perhaps even more revealing that some senators would succumb to your will if you merely dangled the idea of slapping their name on a bridge or airport or federal building.

People were all so—well, self-absorbed, self-centered and parochial. Politics possessed powerful tools, even when you were voting to outlaw an entire race within your country from traveling to their people's homeland. Well, it served the blasted Jews right; they'd been too powerful for too long and felt far too proud of themselves and their accomplishments.

The atmosphere outside the Senate chamber where Fireside stood nearly crackled with electricity. The tension was palpable.

Standing in a wide hallway with gleaming floors and walls soaked with two centuries of rich history, Fireside thought of the consequences. The Party had surely alienated the Jewish vote, but the Muslims with their high birth rate had already overtaken the Jews in numbers, so it was a net win at the polls.

Chuck Claiborne, Fireside's chief of staff, was doing his job, refereeing a scramble of senators trying to get the Vice President's ear.

"Fireside, you'll pay dearly for this. Your career is over!" yelled Senator Bill Bloom.

Fireside looked Bloom directly in the eye and winked, smiled and—the trifecta—shot him a thumbs-up. *Billy-boy, dream on. I just jumped aboard a rocketship, pal.*

Fireside tapped one of his two Secret Service protectors on the shoulder. "Wait here by the door, will you?"

The agent nodded and the two men took up their posts as Fireside escaped to his office just outside the Senate chamber. Fireside stood upright, head back, smiled broadly and walked briskly to his office, closing the door—and the hubbub—behind him. He had to place a most important phone call.

Walking to the double-pedestal, mahogany desk, Fireside wondered how many of his predecessors who had occupied this room could have pulled off this coup. Certainly not its first occupant in 1859, John Breckinridge, the only vice president ever to take up arms against the government of the United States by volunteering his services to the Confederate army even though his cousin Mary Todd Lincoln resided in the White House and his home state of Kentucky remained in the Union.

Certainly not "Cactus Jack," John Nance Garner IV, the Texan for whom the ornately carved rosewood liquor cabinet to Fireside's left was named. Indeed, Garner was no pillar of allegiance himself, breaking with President Franklin Delano Roosevelt over the issue of enlarging the Supreme Court, and helping defeat it on the grounds that it centralized too much power in the President's hands. Garner would invite visitors to "strike a blow for liberty" with the contents of the liquor cabinet. *Yeah, Cactus Jack, where'd that get ya'?*

Not even the brilliant John C. Calhoun, who, after all, evolved into a proponent of states' rights, limited government, nullification and free trade. *Whoa! Where would we be with powerful states' rights and limited government today, not to mention a nullification system under which states could declare null and void federal laws that they viewed as unconstitutional?* Fireside shuddered to think.

Again the question: what Vice President could have pulled off this coup? None, except perhaps LBJ, who, like Fireside, had used this office as an elegant and convenient setting for informal party caucuses, press briefings, ceremonial functions and—ahem, this was the bend-your-arm-'til-it-breaks part—private meetings. LBJ might have been considered the master, but Fireside had just checkmated the big Texan's Gulf of Tonkin Resolution with this Jewish emigration ban.

Yes, Fireside was continuing—indeed, improving on—the history that had been crafted in this room. Until the Russell Senate Office Building opened in 1909, this was only space in Washington assigned to the Vice President, and it served as the sole working office for Teddy Roosevelt, Adlai Stevenson, that great abolotionist Hannibal Hamlin and all the others. It was in this room that Chester A. Arthur took the oath of office as President after the assassination of James Garfield. It was in this room that Vice President Thomas Marshal signed the constitutional amendment grainting nationwide suffrage to women. It was in this room that Vice President Harry S. Truman grabbed his hat to run to the White House and take his oath as President, succeeding FDR who had died.

And in the past few days it was in this room that Fireside had wielded his whip and staff and four-letter-word-laced tongue-lashings to convince a fractious Senate to approve the UN Resolution barring Jews from emigrating to Israel.

Fireside looked down at the circular woolen carpet he had specifically ordered made for this office. Surrounded by the blue of the American flag, in its center a glorious bald eagle with wings outstretched, gripping a scroll of the U.S. Constitution in its talons.

Fireside looked to his left and checked himself out in the ornate gilded mirror that matched the Victorian window cornices dating back to the 19th century. He loosened his tie, smiled at his reflection, then strolled past the marble mantle, over the British-made Minton floor tiles and around behind the historic Wilson desk.

Placing his hands on the desktop, he took a deep

breath, picked up the red telephone and punched in a number he knew well.

•••••

When the phone rang beside him, President Herald Smith switched on a low-wattage bedside lamp. He hadn't been able to sleep, but had fidgeted under the sheets for hours awaiting this call. He had spent his last drop of political capital on this bill, declaring that failure was not an option. Though no one else knew it besides his wife, his future beyond his Presidency hung on its success.

His neck hairs prickled in anticipation. Was it good, news, bad news, or some dire gray-area result? Smith hated gray areas.

Picking up the phone, he answered, "Yes?"

"It's done, Mister President. We're a 'go.'"

Smith's eyes shot wide open and he released an anxiety-laden breath, then asked, "Fallout?"

"Some outrage, plenty of grumble. It's a good thing Lieberman and Shumer are retired. A few almost stalked out of the chambers. Well, Frank and Weiss actually did—as we predicted. That was actually okay because I thought I'd shoot Frank, he was so distraught, so righteous, so—Jewish. We needed a lot of arm-twisting and promises—some of which we really have to talk about today—but, in the end, we avoided insurrection and got it passed. Not by a lot, but it passed."

"Great work, Dan! I'm glad you're at my side in this." Smith rubbed his eyes and seriously considered a drink of hard liquor in celebration as a smile played across his mouth. "It's nice to have a majority in both the House and Senate, isn't it?"

"Agreed."

"You'd better get some rest, my friend."

"I haven't slept in a day and a half. I'll catch a few hours sleep, then meet you in the Oval Office?"

"Right."

"'Night, sir."

"'Night, Dan."

The President turned to his wife, who had sat up beside him.

"The vault door is slammed shut on the Jews," he said with cold certainty. "Last week's vote illegalized removing their fortunes from the country. And now, no longer can they leave America to travel to Israel, or to any country that will allow them to travel to Israel."

In the faint shadows of the room, Theresa Smith smiled back at her husband and whispered hoarsely, "Well done, my love. Besides, what Jew in their right mind would want to go to Israel, what with the Arabs firing rockets at them day and night?"

Smith nodded agreement, then asked, "Like a drink in celebration?"

"In the middle of the night?" Theresa reached for her nightgown hanging on a nearby chair. "Good idea."

Smith swung his feet over the side of the bed and said, "You know when I first saw that this could happen?"

"When?" The First Lady was no won her feet and slipping her feet into slippers.

"Back in August 2014 when the UN Human Rights Commission came down on Israel for *not* sharing its Iron Dome technology with Hamas. That about said everything. Imagine sharing the technology that's saving your lives with the terrorists trying to kill you!"

"M-hm. Shows how much the folks at the UN hate the Jews."

"And they're not alone," Smith said. "Gin and tonic?"

His wife nodded. "You know me so well, Mister President."

·····

An uneasiness he could not explain had urged Bunyan "Jacko" Jackson from his bed to the patio at the rear of his oceanside estate. He stood—all six-foot-four inches and two hundred and thirty-four pounds of him—with his hands on the waist-high railing, peering out onto the dark Atlantic Ocean beyond his expansive lawn.

He was dressed in lightweight pajamas, with a flimsy cotton robe pulled about him. It was a warm summer night on the outskirts of Portland, Maine. The nightglow of the city to the north turned the sky a pale fluorescent green. The faint smell of salt water told him the tide was out.

Just then he heard the first couple bars of Louis Armstrong's *What a Wonderful World* on his cell phone through an open window in his bedroom. He hustled over the planks of his wide deck and through the patio door into his room, wondering who was in the hospital, or who had died, or what else on earth would cause a call at this hour.

Picking up his phone stopped the music and he answered, "Jackson."

"My friend, it's me." The distinctive Israeli accent of Omri Zohn made Jackson stand straight in anticipation. "*Aliyah* is on. Plan B."

Click.

Jackson's mouth went wide. He scowled at the phone in his hand as if it were a grenade, or an implement that could answer the stark questions: How could we? How could the United States do this to its own people? Have we not learned from what we did to the Japanese Americans during the Second World War? Have we not learned from slavery? Have we finally succumbed to an Islamic-driven United Nations gone rogue?

In dismay, he said, "Well, Satchmo, today's it's not such a 'wonderful world.'" He laid the phone down on the bedside table and sat down on the king-size bed. He inhaled deeply and peered at a shelf below the tabletop. Reaching down, he pulled out a leather-bound copy of *The Pilgrim's Progress* that had been handed down by his Great-great-great-great-grandfather Tice, who had escaped slavery in 1860. The book was an allegory of a man's journey from the City of Destruction, the world, through all sorts of obstacles and diversions to the Celestial City, heaven. It was the book from which Tice had learned to read and taken to heart deep things of God.

Jackson thought of the book's story, then recalled the passage in the 9th chapter of the Book of Amos: "I will bring back My exiled people Israel…"

This was it: the last *aliyah*. And here he was—retired Major League baseball player, Hall of Famer and descendant of a slave—positioned to pay forward what so many good-minded people had done for Tice. Jackson brought the little book to his lips for a light kiss. "We'll get them to Jerusalem. I promise, Grampa Tice."

Setting the book down, Jackson picked up a thick, well-worn manuscript in a homemade binder—Tice's hand-written account of his own escape from the South. With a deep love of an ancestor he had never met, Bunyan frowned sadly at the thought that the world had come to this. He stood and walked to a two-shelf glassed-in bookcase and pulled out a world atlas. Opening it up revealed a PGP mobile phone hidden in a hollow. He grabbed the phone and texted in an encypted message that when deciphered read: *"Aliyah is on. Plan B."*

•••••

Ethan and Naomi Rosenbaum lay sound asleep in their comfortable gambrel in a comfortable neighborhood in the comfortable city of Charleston, South Carolina.

Ethan was engrossed in a dream. He was standing beside an enormous aerosol can nearly as tall as his six-foot height and waiting on the platform of a railway station, Naomi at his side. Brutish men, their muscles bulging in Nazi SS uniforms, beat nightsticks against their bare palms and stalked back and forth, scowling and demanding that all Jews step to the edge of the platform. Naomi looked at Ethan in fear. He smiled back, moved her gently in front of the aerosol can and pulled down on its actuator. A vapor from the can enveloped Naomi and she vanished from sight. Ethan then slid into the spot where Naomi had stood and was reaching up to depress the valve when one of his colleagues at his company's research and development department appeared a few feet away. A tall, thin, blonde-haired and blue-eyed woman, she called out to an SS officer and pointed at Ethan, "There's one!" she cried. "There's a Jew!"

Ethan jerked awake at the same moment the telephone on his bedside table rang with an old-fashioned jingle.

He pushed himself to a sitting position, opened an eye to look at his oversized clock, groaned and reluctantly picked up the phone.

"Aliyah is on," said the Israeli-tinted voice. "Plan B, ASAP."

Click.

Ethan's eyes shot all the way open but he sat motionless, as if his body had been shot with Novacane, trying to absorb the impact of the news. He remembered as a fullback being flattened by a huge defensive tackle in a high school football game. This was like that, only emotionally. No broken bones, just a shattered spirit.

Since the United Nations had voted for the extraordinary Resolution stopping all Jewish immigration to Israel, he had entertained thoughts of what would happen if, God forbid, Congress were to vote in agreement. Once, this possibility had been unimaginable. Over the years the Palestinian-friendly United Nations had passed so many anti-Israel Resolutions that had come to naught that they were normally thought of as simple bluster; plus the United States had usually used its veto power against any measures that would physically harm Israel.

It had been common knowledge for several decades that the State Department was anti-Semitic and anti-Zionist, even withholding recognition of Jerusalem as Israel's capital. But few had actually believed America and other countries around the world would acquiesce when it came to enforcement of this type of Resolution. Had they?

Yet, America's government seemed like the antithesis of an elephant; it remembered nothing, learned no lessons. Over the years, although the United States had earkmarked nearly two-thirds of its $30-billion-plus annual foreign aid to Muslim nations and one-third to Arab countries, those nations voted against America's will anywhere from 67 to 87 percent of the time, depending on the country. Egypt, Jordan, Pakistan? All receiving billions from America, all voting against the United States nearly all of the time.

But America continued mailing out those checks, like a senior citizen paying life insurance premiums for a spouse who was long dead.

But now this Resolution had proven not only possible but a done deal. Instead of voting "No" at the UN, the United States had abstained. Yes, since then the country had been abuzz, but not inflamed—not like it would have been five, ten years ago. And whatever power the American Jewish Congress, the Anti-Defamation League, B'nai B'rith, Jewish Defense League and other organizations had swayed in the past had waned in the enslaught of media demnation for everything Jewish.

It seemed that whenever Israel's government had vanquished their own people from their homes and handed the land over to the Palestinians, Hezbollah and Hamaz had moved in to set up new rocket-launching sites to pulverize Jewish towns. And the world, Americans included, yawned. *Nothing happening here. Move on.* Whenever the Israelis released scores of Arabs imprisoned for murder—even mass murder—the world, Americans included, yawned. *Nothing happening here. Move on.*

And so now, in the wake of the UN Resolution, the Jewish and Christian outrage obviously paled to the "hoorahs" of the anti-Semites and anti-Zionists and failed to dissuade Congress.

Ethan and his wife Naomi had toyed with the idea of what they would do if this moment happened. But he had considered those thoughts simple fantasy because, really, how could America, "home of the free because of the brave," abide by such a decision? Surely there would be rebellion in the streets. Right?

Nevertheless, he and Omri Zohn had devised various plans for *aliyah*—just in case. That's what scientists do: devise tests, plans and contingencies for various scenarios. Another thing scientists do: harden themselves to believe provable facts, no matter the substance or depth of information indicating the contrary. They had a Plan A for Monday through Thursday and a Plan B for midnight Thursday through Sunday.

At his side, Naomi stirred awake. "What is it, Ethan? Who was that?"

"Congress." He hesitated and swallowed hard. "It's lost its collective mind."

His response jolted his wife fully awake and she shot up out of the sheets. "No!" she cried.

"That call was from Omri," he said. "They did it. Congress sold us out."

Naomi released a long breath and spoke as if in wonder, "They can't see the iceberg."

"Iceberg?"

"The iceberg that threatens to sink this country if Congress took this vote," she said. "For God himself declared, 'I will bless those who bless my people, but those who curse them, I will curse.'"

ENDNOTES

Slavery. Some called it "The absolute power of one person over another—the vilest human behavior and institution."

But others called it "essential to our economy and prosperity and at the same time a humane institution which provided food, shelter and daily to an inferior race."

James Fenimore Cooper went so far as to say that for the Negro, "slavery has made him, from a savage, an orderly and efficient laborer. It supports him in comfort and peace. It restrains his vices. It improves his kind, orals and manners."

Slavery was the one issue that has been able to tear our nation apart—the fight to preserve it and the battle to undo its entangling web of depravity.

My tale of Tice's escape from a plantation in Kentucky is just one route a slave could take in 1860, each one packed with danger, looming calamity and, often, death. And each slave's escape route could be unique. Indeed, in Maine alone there were 71 "stops" on the Underground Railroad.

In the opening scene, slaves are singing the Negro spiritual Swing Low, Sweet Chariot which the black slaves saw as referring to a house in Ripley, Ohio, on the northern shore of the Ohio River whose mistress kept a lantern burning to lead escaping slaves to their protection. A number of prominent abolitionists lived in the town in the 1800s, mainly along the river where Tice swam across.

In fact, my inspiration for Tice came from a slave named Tice Davids, who escaped from a plantation in

Maysville, Kentucky, plunging into the Ohio River and swimming to Ripley, with his master close on his heels via ferry.

Small groups in towns and cities north of the Mason-Dixon Line, insisting that slavery laws defied the law of God which declares that all men are brothers, banded together to help runaway slaves. If caught, a person helping a slave faced a jail sentence and heavy fine.

Several of True North's characters were real people, black and white, putting their lives and fortunes on the line… Henry David Thoreau; Jonathan Ball and the Jacksons in Newton, Massachusetts; Thoreau's Indian friend Joe; Reuben Ruby and the Fessendens in Portland, Maine; the Nasons in Augusta, Maine; the Chadbournes in Vassalboro, Maine; the Holyokes in Brewer, Maine; and, of course, Hannibal Hamlin, the Bangor, Maine abolitionist whom Abraham Lincoln chose as his running mate to be Vice President.

Other characters are composites, like Tice's friend Freeborn, who had been a slave in a mine. (Not all slaves worked the plantations.)

Heroes abounded. Black and white. People of different faiths. Both north and south of the Mason-Dixon Line.

Canada was the safe haven, so all the Underground Railroads ran north or northeast—the North Star being the slaves' guide.

My character Tice's trail led ever northeastward to Maine. Specifically Portland, Augusta, Vassalboro, Bangor, Brewer and northward on the Penobscot River.

Portland was famous for what is now called the Portland Freedom Trail, whose memory is kept alive by an impressive group of citizens. Interested people can investigate it at www.portlandfreedomtrail.org.

Today, most of the landmarks on the Trail are

simple raised bronze plaques, marking the spots of the Mariners' Church, Fessenden House, Reuben Ruby and Charles H.L. Pierre's hack stands, Jacob C. Dickson's Barber Shp and others once stood. Others still stand, notably the Franklin Street Wharf, the Nathaniel Dow House on Congress Street, and the Abyssinian Church which is undergoing massive reconstruction on Newberry Street.

By and large, True North's characters were real people, black and white, putting their lives and fortunes on the line. And, indeed, slave hunters scoured the wharfs, churches and homes of Portland because it was a major shipping town and, therefore, place of departure by ship for a number of runaways.

Not to be lost in the discussion of the slavery era and "restitution" is that, while 299,524 men died fighting for the South, the Northern Union Army suffered 364,511 dead—mostly white men battling to free their black brethren. My wife and I both have ancestors who put their lives on the line to keep the United States of America united and free the slaves.

Chronology of the Underground Railroad

1746 — Quaker moralist John Woolman influences Quakers to break with the American slavery system.

1783 — Nova Scotia welcomes the first sizable community of former slaves when the Black Pioneers regiment, led by Thomas Peters and Murphy Still, receives free land and builds the communities of Shelburne and Birchtown, home to 3,000 refugees.

July 9, 1793 — After Lieutenant Governor John Graves Simcoe abolishes slavery in the Canadian provinces, Canada becomes a magnet for runaways from the United States.

1804 — By 1804, all states north of Maryland have abolished slavery.

1820 — House Speaker Henry Clay of Kentucky and Senator Jesse B. Thomas of Illinois agree upon the Missouri Compromise, an accord that limits the geographical spread of slavery, allowing admission of Missouri to the Union as a slave state only after Maine is admitted as a free state.

January 1, 1831 — William Lloyd Garrison begins publishing a weekly abolitionist newspaper, The Liberator, a resource and sounding board for Underground Railroad agents.

August 1831 — After the Nat Turner rebellion in Southampton, Virginia, results in the slaughter of 60 whites and more than 200 blacks, Southerners institute restrictive Black Laws, step up patrols, and hire spies to divulge pockets of slave harboring in mid-Atlantic and Midwestern states.

December 4-6, 1833 — The American Anti-Slavery Society replaces the haphazard rescues by a few unorganized abolitionist cells with teams of volunteers and a sophisticated detection and spy system.

1842 — The ruling of the U.S. Supreme Court in Prigg v. Pennsylvania declares that the 1793 Fugitive Slave Law supersedes state statutes overriding federal law; however, it frees states from mandatory arrest and jailing of black refugees.

1851-1852 — The National Era serializes Harriet Beecher Stowe's Uncle Tom's Cabin, a fictionalized account of the rescue work of Jean Lowry Rankin and John Rankin, Underground Railroad conductors in Ripley, Ohio.

April 12, 1861 — Diametric arguments concerning slavery lead to the American Civil War.

Jan. 1, 1863 — After Abraham Lincoln issues the Emancipation Proclamation, agent Thomas Wentworth Higginson chooses conductor William Henry Brisbane to read the document aloud to a collection of dignitaries and the Eighth Maine Regiment in Port Royal, South Carolina.

1865 — Famed Underground Railroad spy John T. Hanover of Indiana reports that 4,000 runaways per year received Underground Railroad transportation in the 15 years following passage of the Fugitive Slave Act of 1850.

Passage of the Thirteenth Amendment to the U.S. Constitution removes the need for an Underground Railroad by outlawing slavery.

Other Books by Mark Alan Leslie

Midnight Rider for the Morning Star, published by the Francis Asbury Press, Wilmore, Ky., 2008
2nd printing 2014
Available in softcover at www.amazon.com and Francis Asbury Press, P.O. Box 7, Wilmore, Ky. 40390
Available as an e-book at www.amazon.com and www.barnesandnoble.com

Fired? Get Fired Up, published as an e-book and available at www.amazon.com and www.barnesandnoble.com, 2009

Walks with God: A Devotional, published as an e-book and available at www.amazon.com and www.barnesandnoble.com, 2010

Putting a Little Spin on It: The Design's the Thing!, published as an e-book and available at www.amazon.com and www.barnesandnoble.com, 2013

Putting a Little Spin on It: The Grooming's the Thing!, published as an e-book and available at www.amazon.com and www.barnesandnoble.com, 2014

Contact

Mark Alan Leslie is a longtime journalist who has won five national magazine writing awards. He lives in Maine with his wife, Loy, and they have two adult children.

Leslie is available to speak at historical societies, libraries, schools, churches and other venues.

He can be contacted at:
30 Ridge Road
Monmouth, ME
USA   04259
T. 207-933-2480
C. 207-312-4495
E-mail: gripfast@roadrunner.com
Web: www.markalanleslie.com

CPSIA information can be obtained at www.ICGtesting.com
Printed in the USA
LVOW12s0406190515

439010LV00023B/502/P